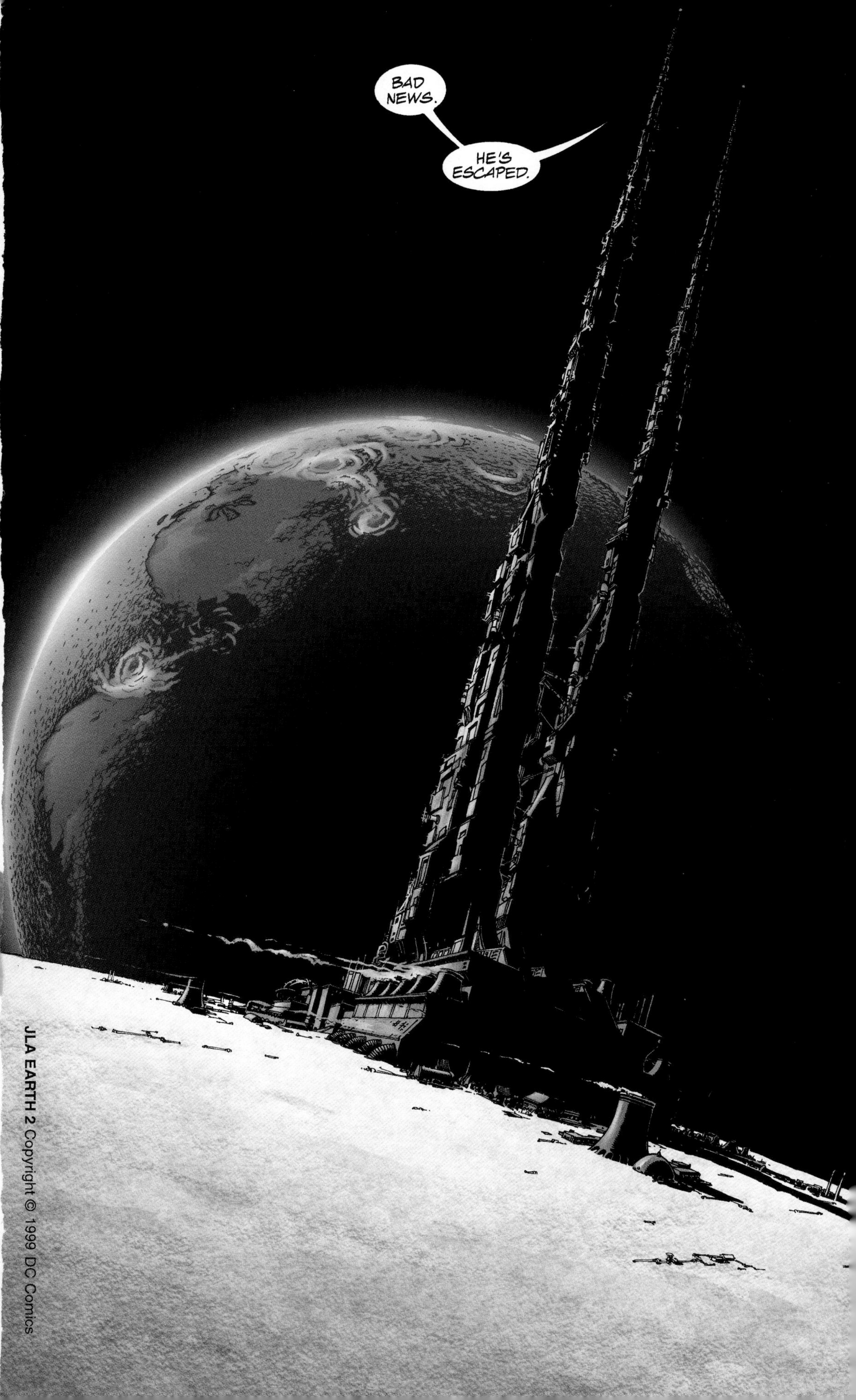
BAD NEWS.
HE'S ESCAPED.

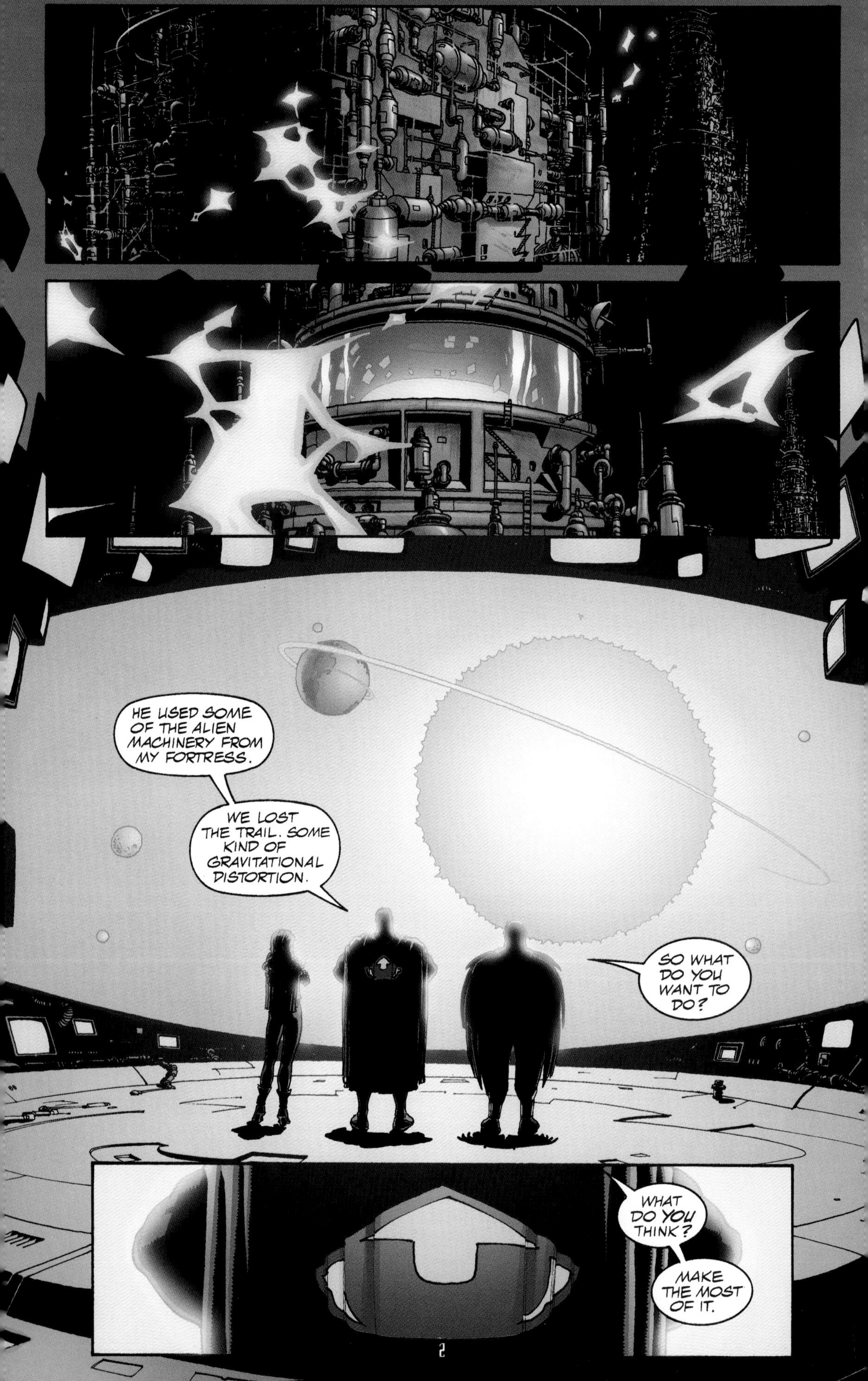
HE USED SOME OF THE ALIEN MACHINERY FROM MY FORTRESS.
WE LOST THE TRAIL. SOME KIND OF GRAVITATIONAL DISTORTION.
SO WHAT DO YOU WANT TO DO?
WHAT DO YOU THINK?
MAKE THE MOST OF IT.

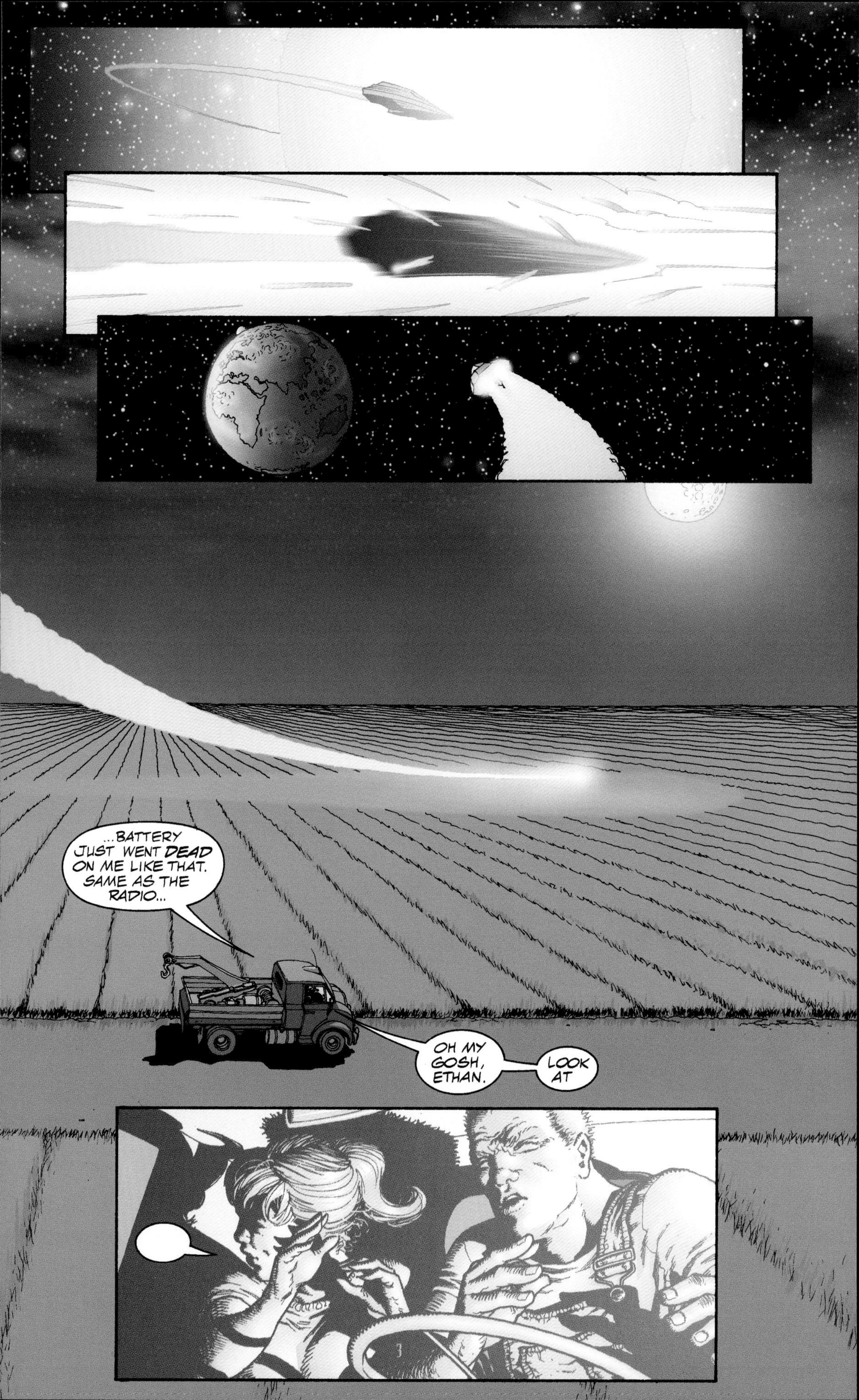
...BATTERY JUST WENT *DEAD* ON ME LIKE THAT. SAME AS THE RADIO...
OH MY GOSH, ETHAN.
LOOK AT

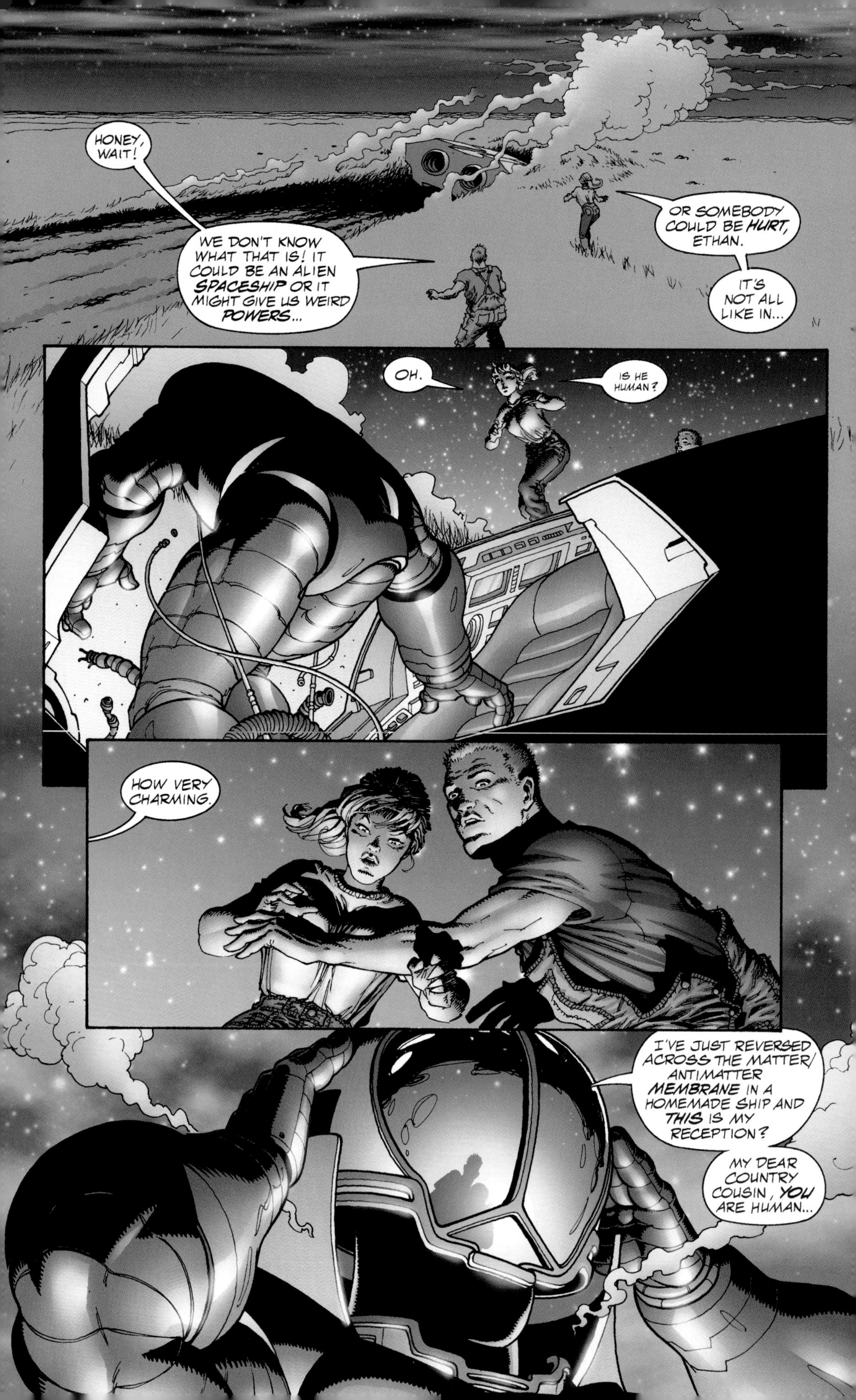
HONEY, WAIT!
WE DON'T KNOW WHAT THAT IS! IT COULD BE AN ALIEN SPACESHIP OR IT MIGHT GIVE US WEIRD POWERS...
OR SOMEBODY COULD BE HURT, ETHAN.
IT'S NOT ALL LIKE IN...
OH.
IS HE HUMAN?
HOW VERY CHARMING.
I'VE JUST REVERSED ACROSS THE MATTER/ ANTIMATTER MEMBRANE IN A HOMEMADE SHIP AND THIS IS MY RECEPTION?
MY DEAR COUNTRY COUSIN, YOU ARE HUMAN...

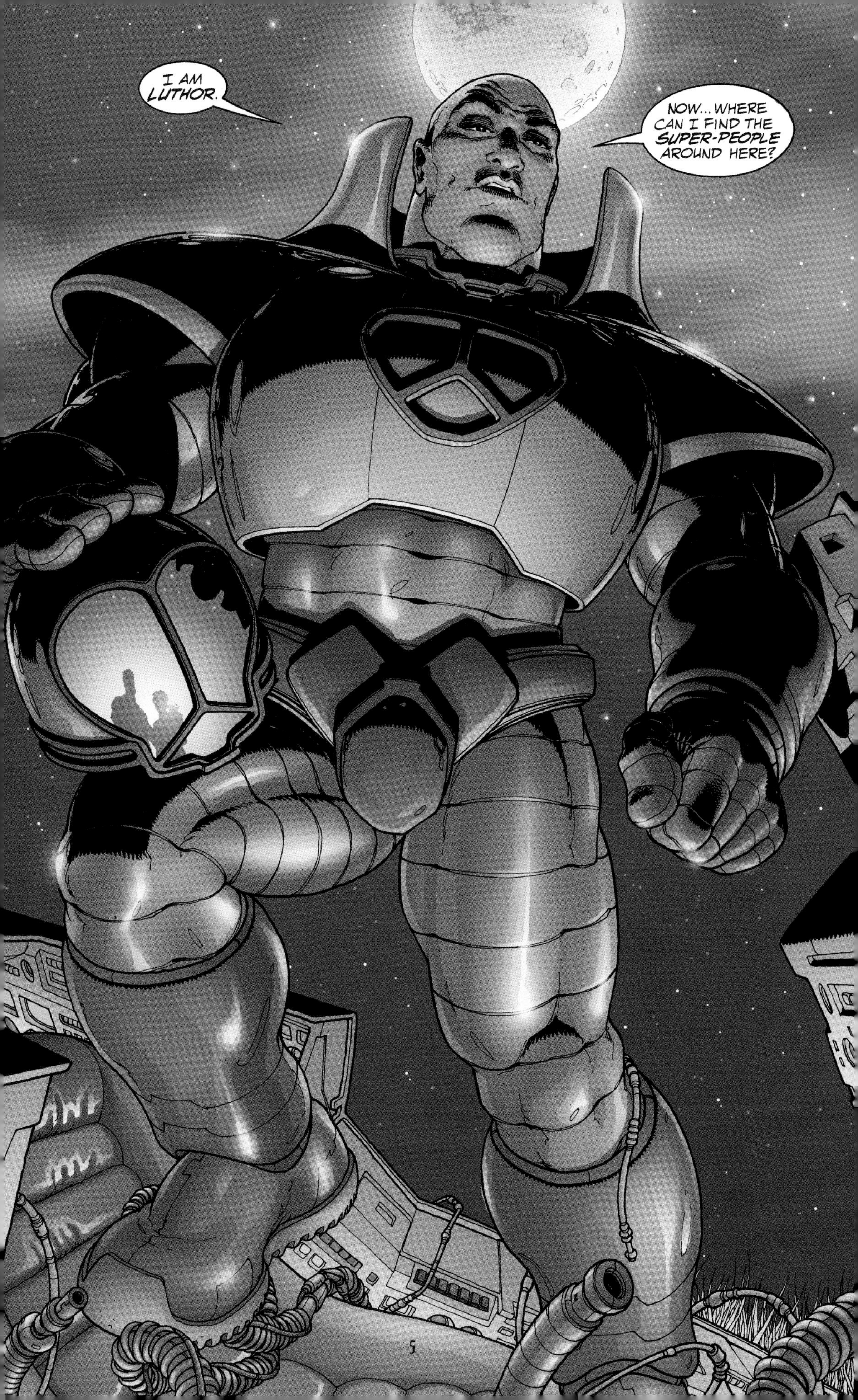
I AM LUTHOR.
NOW... WHERE CAN I FIND THE SUPER-PEOPLE AROUND HERE?

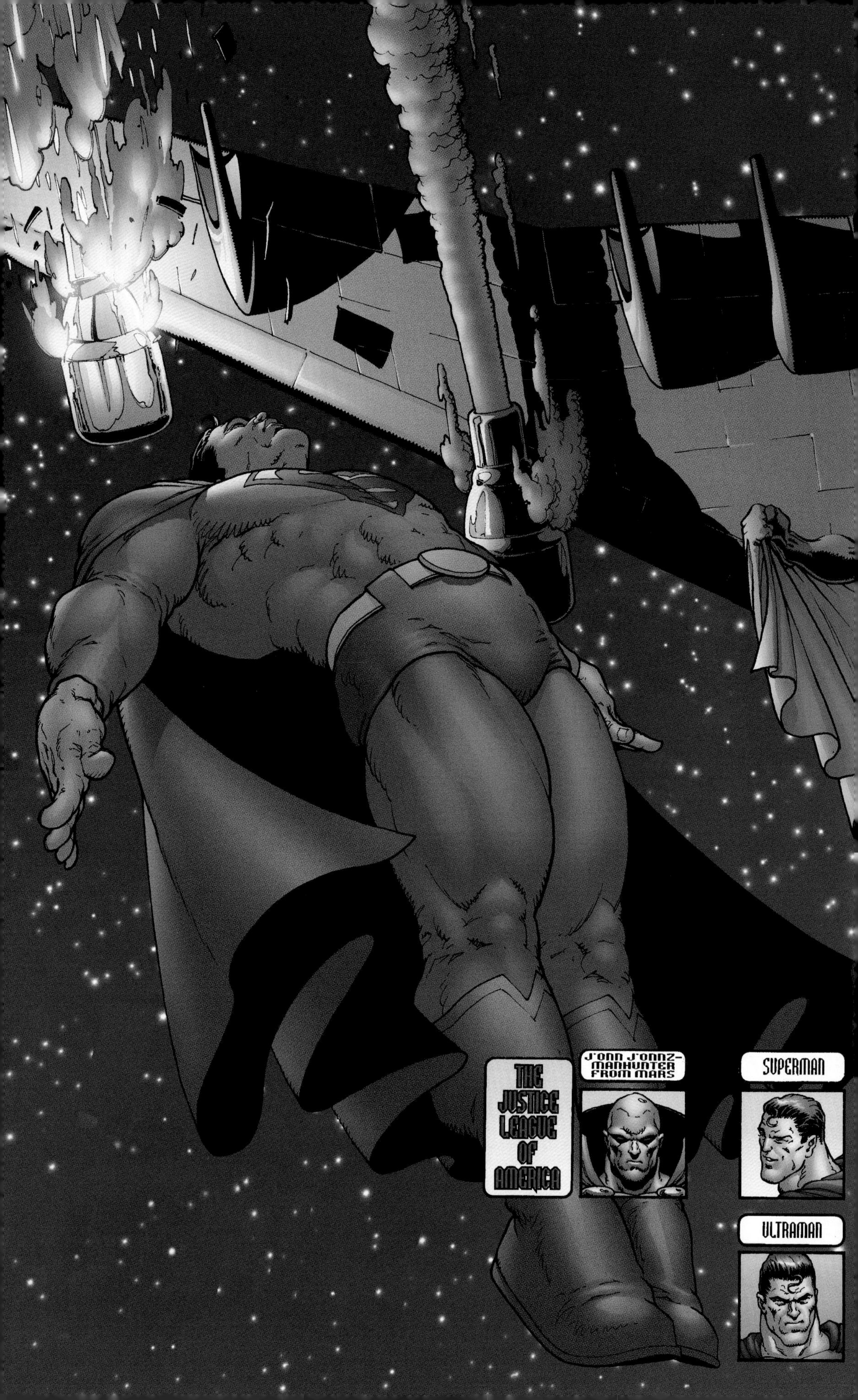
THE JUSTICE LEAGUE OF AMERICA
J'ONN J'ONZZ-MANHUNTER FROM MARS
SUPERMAN
ULTRAMAN

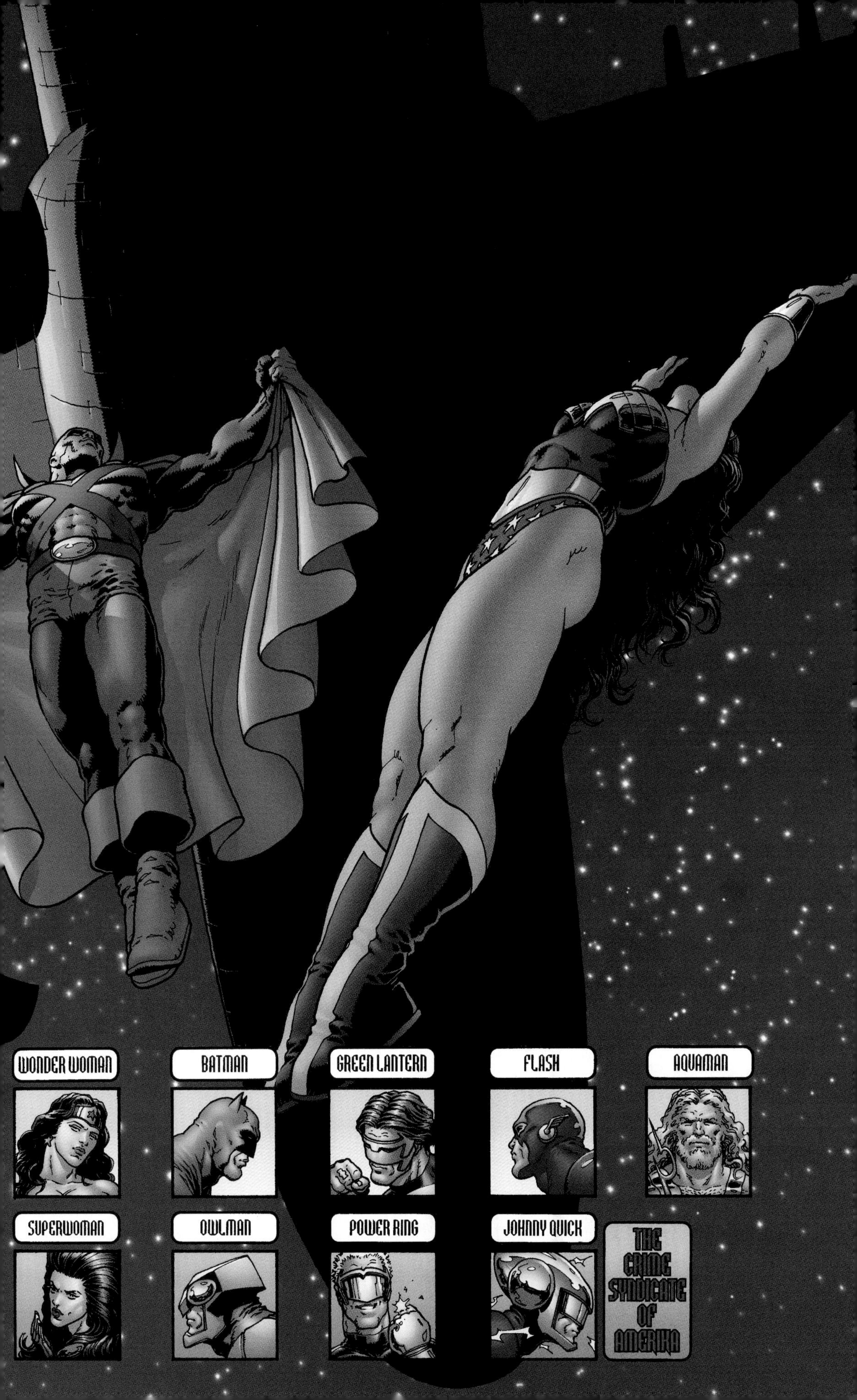
WONDER WOMAN
BATMAN
GREEN LANTERN
FLASH
AQUAMAN
SUPERWOMAN
OWLMAN
POWER RING
JOHNNY QUICK
THE CRIME SYNDICATE OF AMERIKA

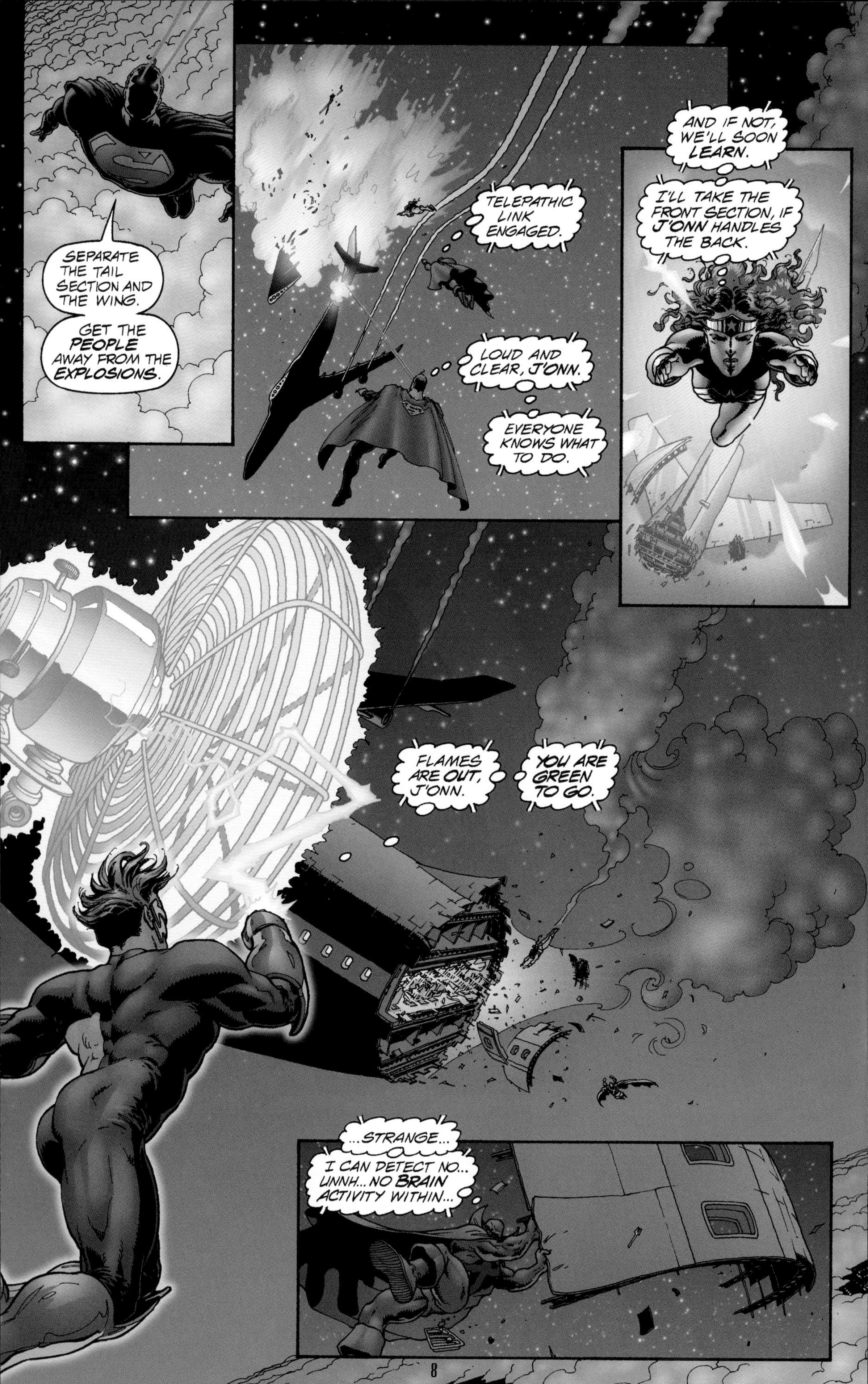
SEPARATE THE TAIL SECTION AND THE WING.
GET THE PEOPLE AWAY FROM THE EXPLOSIONS.
TELEPATHIC LINK ENGAGED.
LOUD AND CLEAR, J'ONN.
EVERYONE KNOWS WHAT TO DO.
AND IF NOT, WE'LL SOON LEARN.
I'LL TAKE THE FRONT SECTION, IF J'ONN HANDLES THE BACK.
FLAMES ARE OUT, J'ONN.
YOU ARE GREEN TO GO.
...STRANGE...
I CAN DETECT NO... UNNH... NO BRAIN ACTIVITY WITHIN...

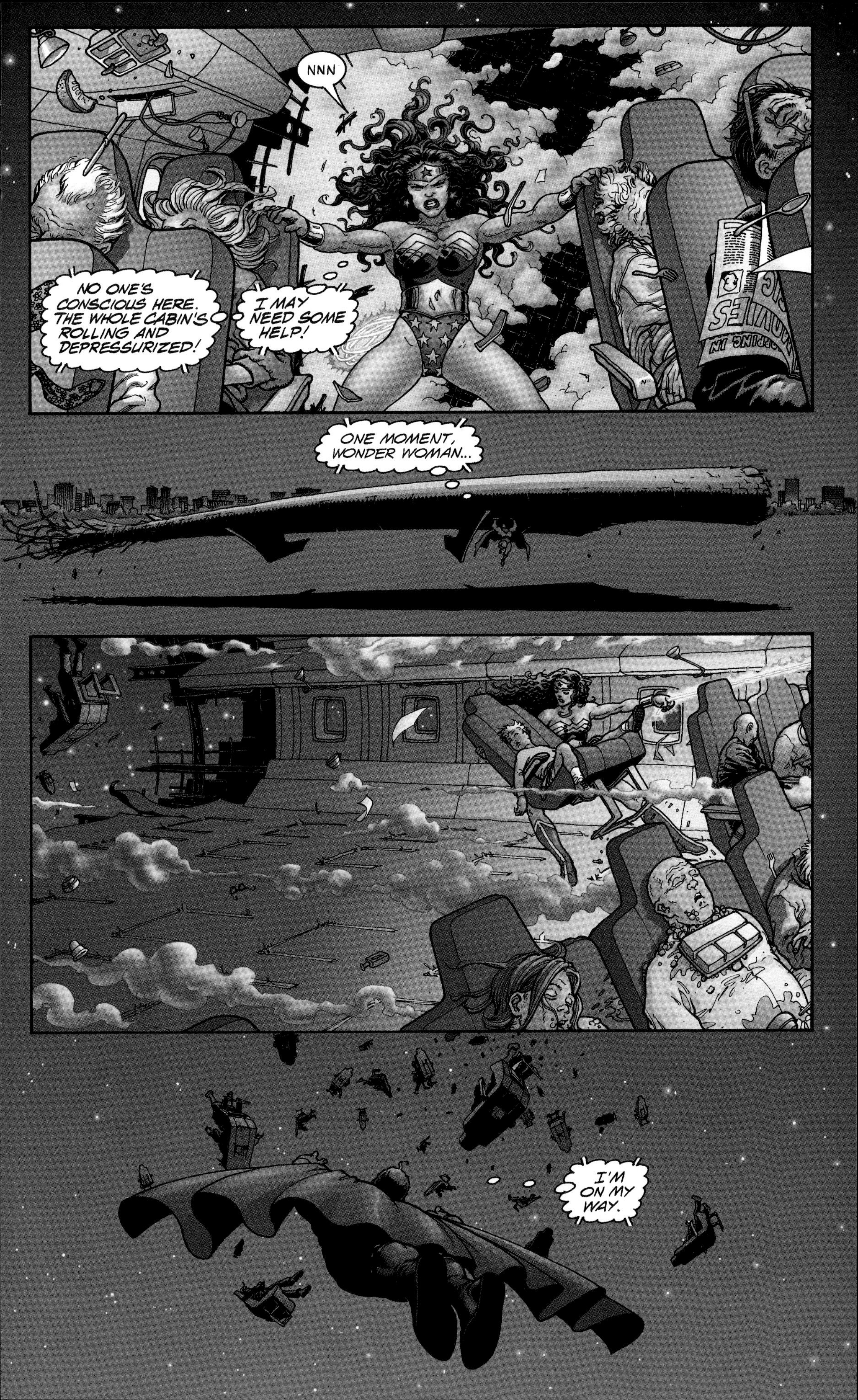
NNN
NO ONE'S CONSCIOUS HERE. THE WHOLE CABIN'S ROLLING AND DEPRESSURIZED!
I MAY NEED SOME HELP!
ONE MOMENT, WONDER WOMAN...
I'M ON MY WAY.

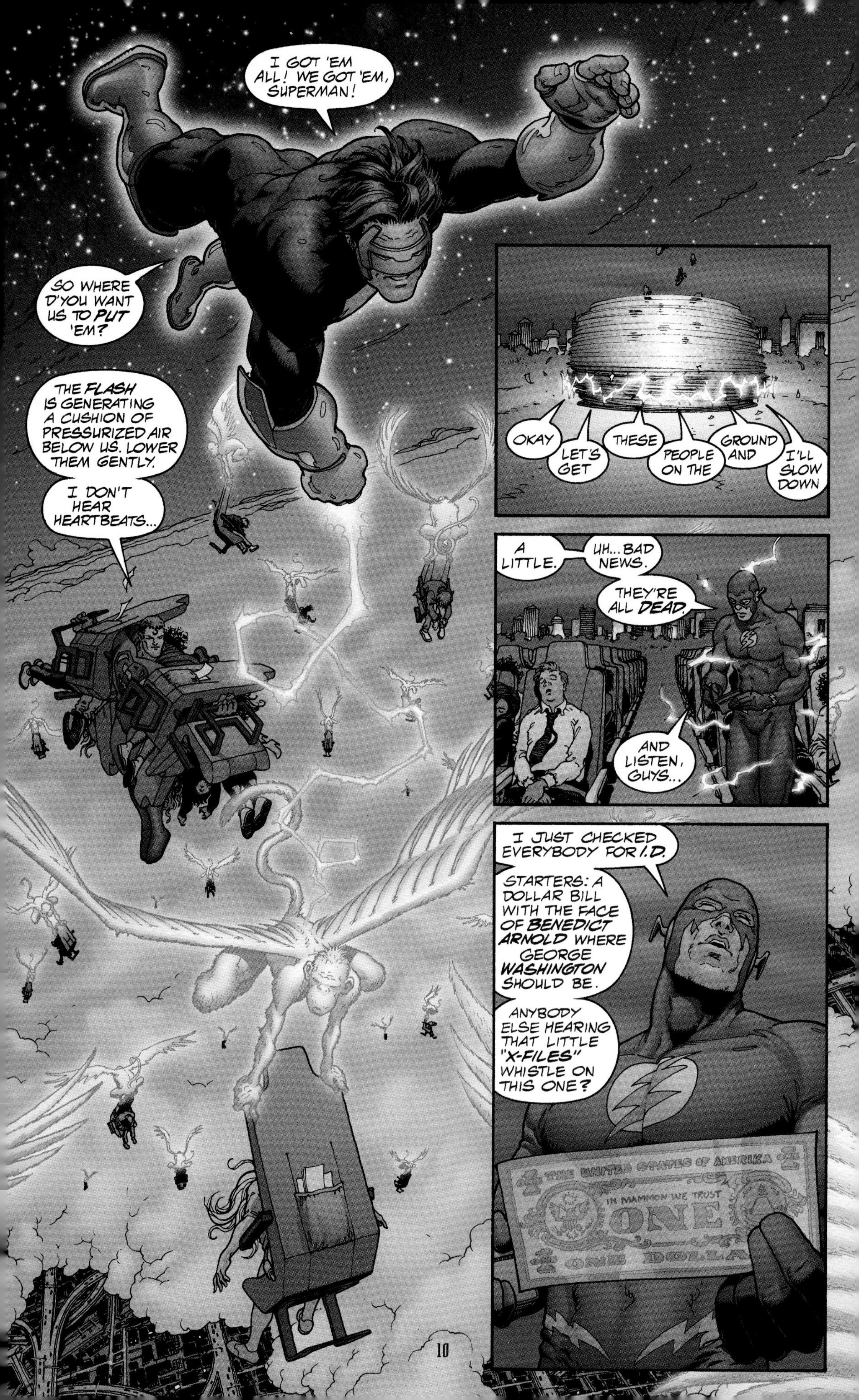
I GOT 'EM ALL! WE GOT 'EM, SUPERMAN!
SO WHERE D'YOU WANT US TO PUT 'EM?
THE FLASH IS GENERATING A CUSHION OF PRESSURIZED AIR BELOW US. LOWER THEM GENTLY.
I DON'T HEAR HEARTBEATS...
OKAY
LET'S GET
THESE
PEOPLE ON THE
GROUND AND
I'LL SLOW DOWN
A LITTLE.
UH... BAD NEWS.
THEY'RE ALL DEAD.
AND LISTEN, GUYS...
I JUST CHECKED EVERYBODY FOR I.D.
STARTERS: A DOLLAR BILL WITH THE FACE OF BENEDICT ARNOLD WHERE GEORGE WASHINGTON SHOULD BE.
ANYBODY ELSE HEARING THAT LITTLE "X-FILES" WHISTLE ON THIS ONE?
THE UNITED STATES OF AMERIKA
IN MAMMON WE TRUST
ONE
ONE DOLLA

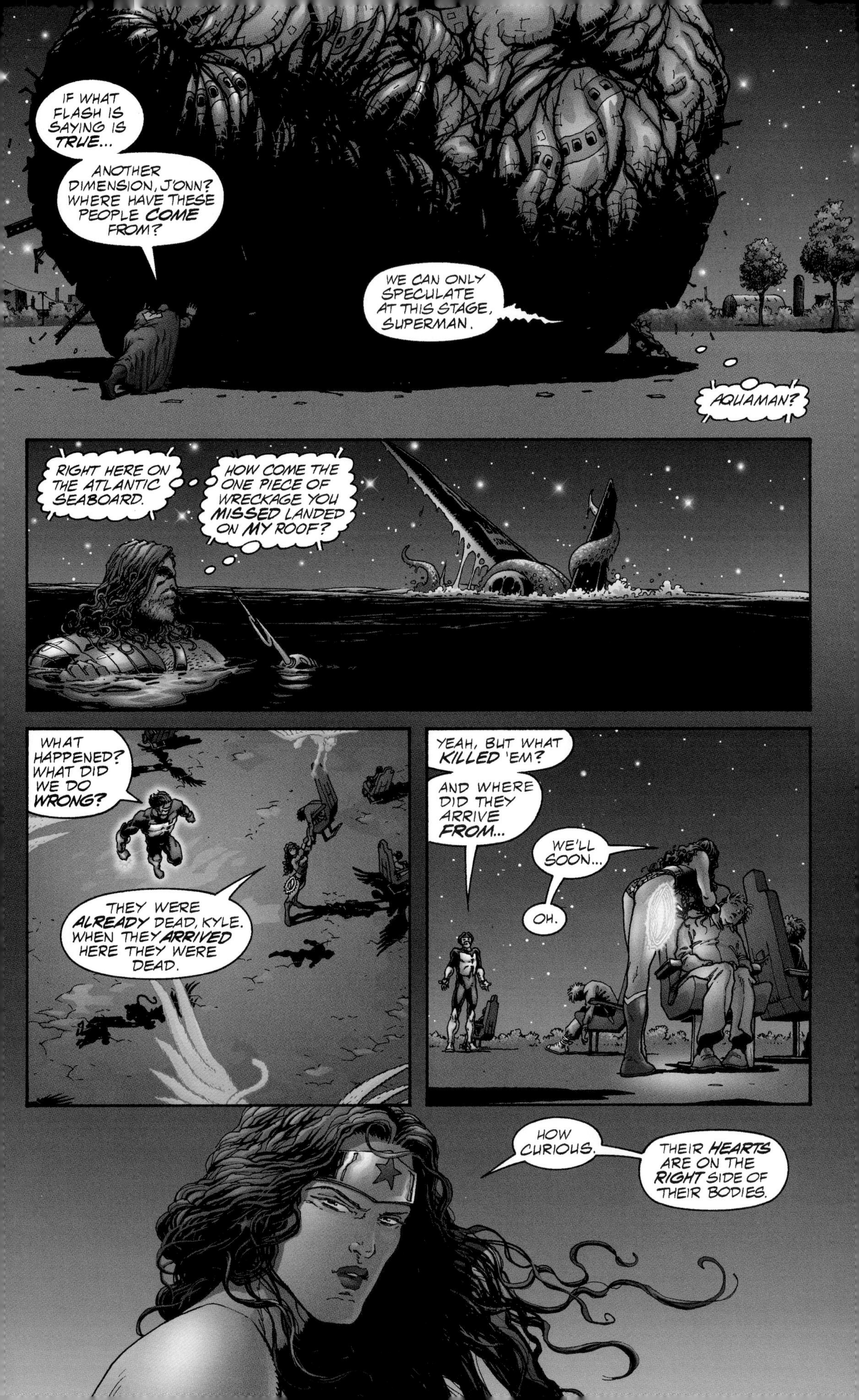
IF WHAT FLASH IS SAYING IS TRUE...
ANOTHER DIMENSION, J'ONN? WHERE HAVE THESE PEOPLE COME FROM?
WE CAN ONLY SPECULATE AT THIS STAGE, SUPERMAN.
AQUAMAN?
RIGHT HERE ON THE ATLANTIC SEABOARD.
HOW COME THE ONE PIECE OF WRECKAGE YOU MISSED LANDED ON MY ROOF?
WHAT HAPPENED? WHAT DID WE DO WRONG?
THEY WERE ALREADY DEAD, KYLE. WHEN THEY ARRIVED HERE THEY WERE DEAD.
YEAH, BUT WHAT KILLED 'EM?
AND WHERE DID THEY ARRIVE FROM...
WE'LL SOON...
OH.
HOW CURIOUS.
THEIR HEARTS ARE ON THE RIGHT SIDE OF THEIR BODIES.

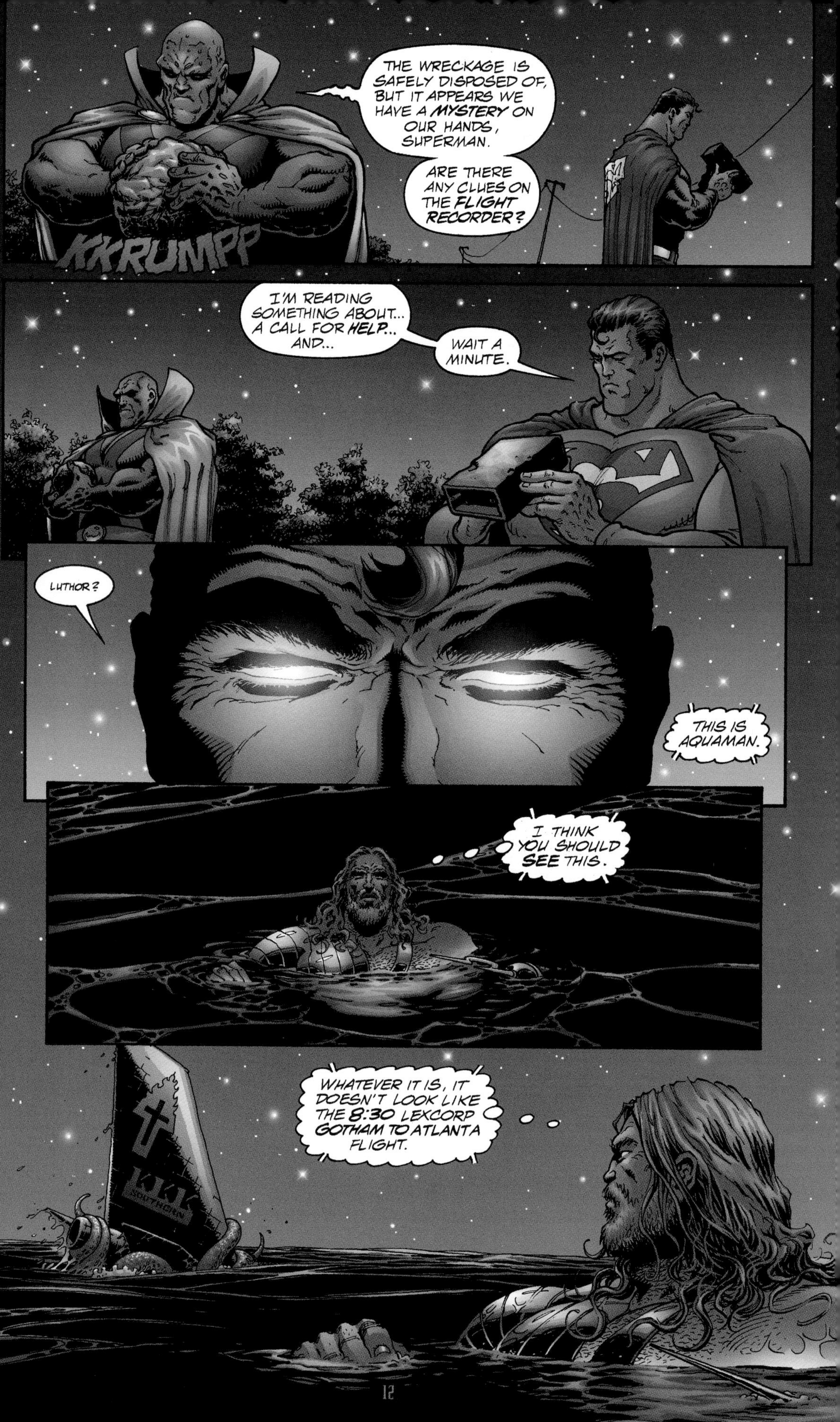

THE WRECKAGE IS SAFELY DISPOSED OF, BUT IT APPEARS WE HAVE A MYSTERY ON OUR HANDS, SUPERMAN.
ARE THERE ANY CLUES ON THE FLIGHT RECORDER?
KKRUMPP
I'M READING SOMETHING ABOUT... A CALL FOR HELP... AND...
WAIT A MINUTE.
LUTHOR?
THIS IS AQUAMAN.
I THINK YOU SHOULD SEE THIS.
WHATEVER IT IS, IT DOESN'T LOOK LIKE THE 8:30 LEXCORP GOTHAM TO ATLANTA FLIGHT.

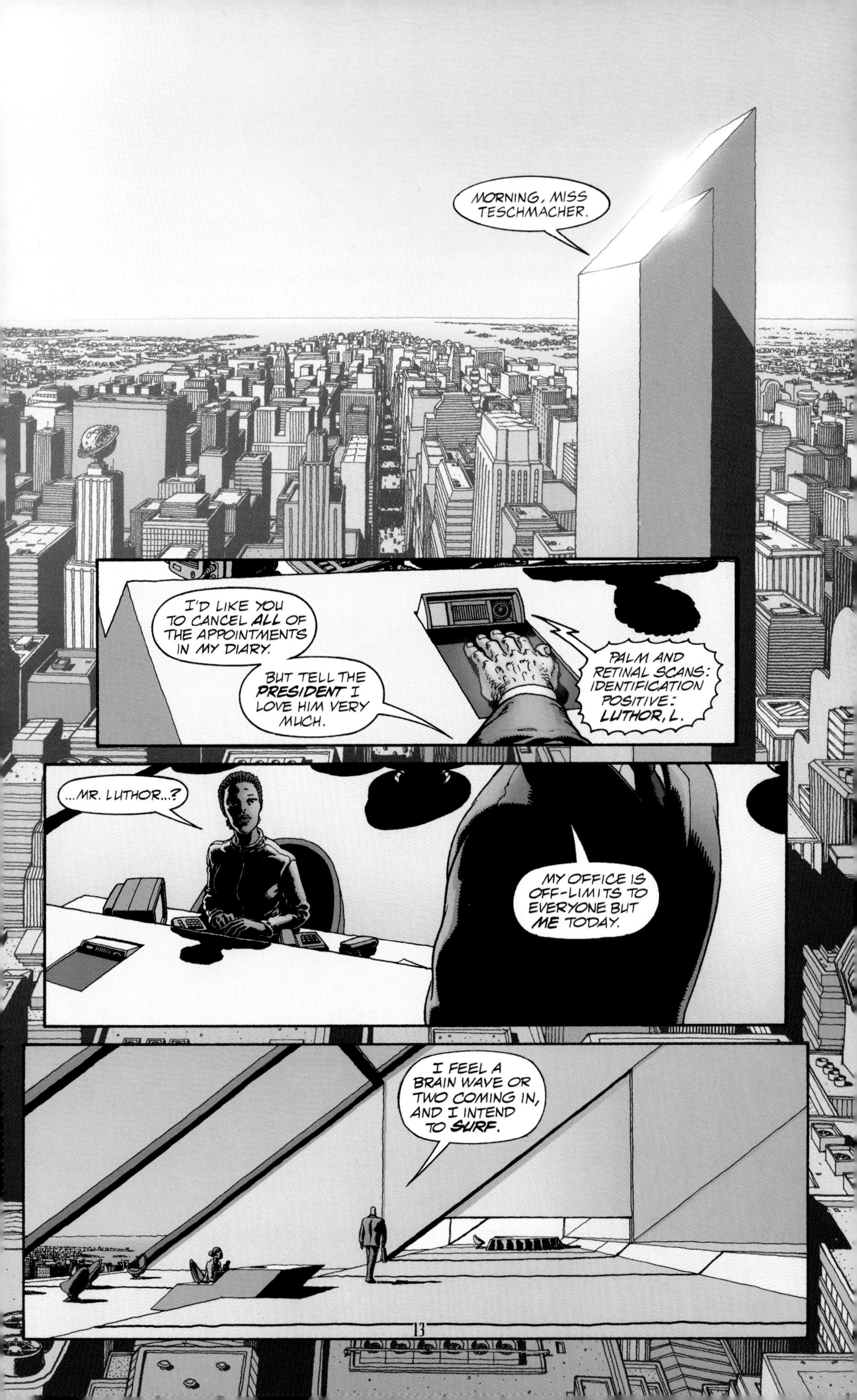
MORNING, MISS TESCHMACHER.
I'D LIKE YOU TO CANCEL ALL OF THE APPOINTMENTS IN MY DIARY.
BUT TELL THE PRESIDENT I LOVE HIM VERY MUCH.
PALM AND RETINAL SCANS: IDENTIFICATION POSITIVE: LUTHOR, L.
...MR. LUTHOR...?
MY OFFICE IS OFF-LIMITS TO EVERYONE BUT ME TODAY.
I FEEL A BRAIN WAVE OR TWO COMING IN, AND I INTEND TO SURF.

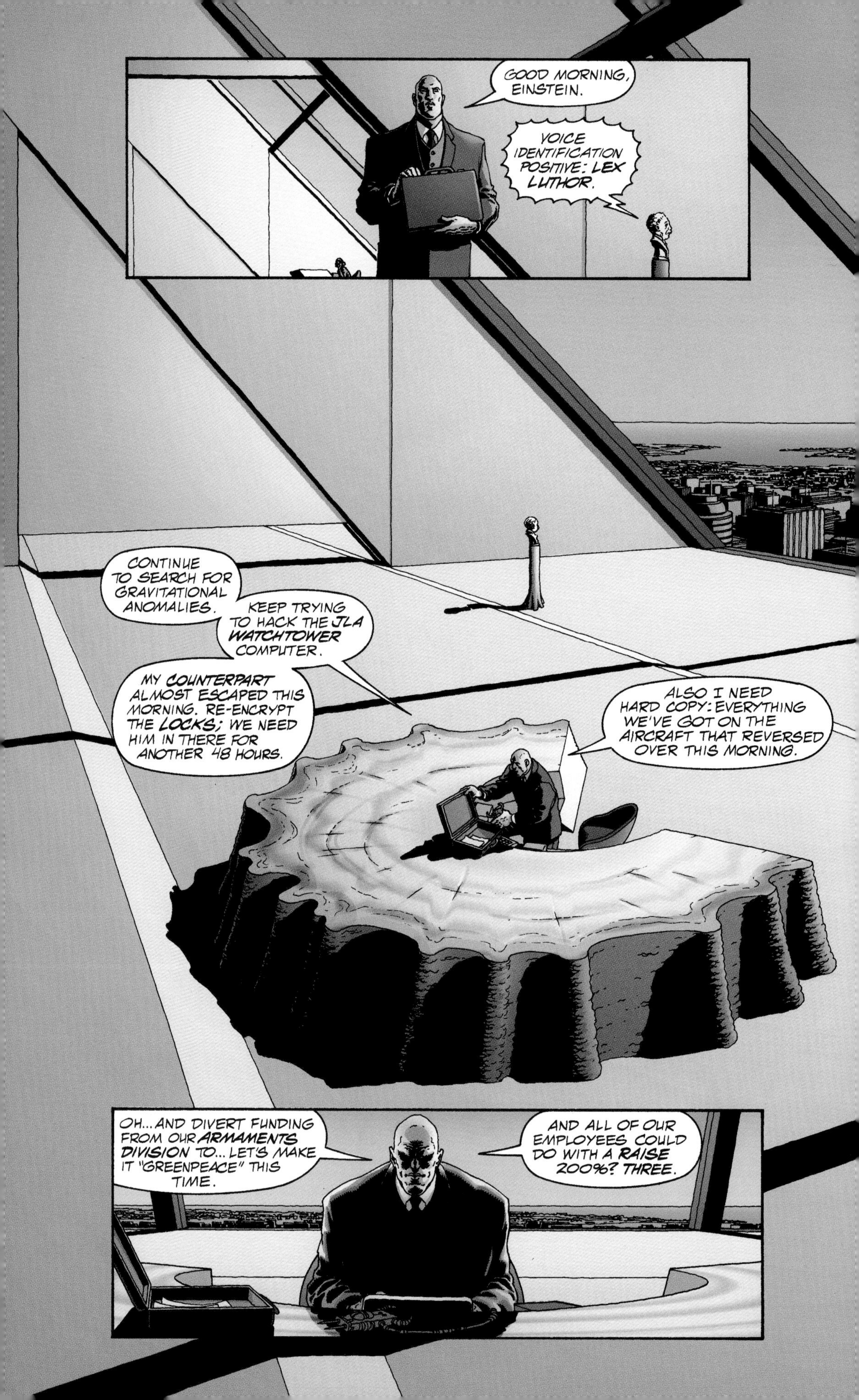
GOOD MORNING, EINSTEIN.
VOICE IDENTIFICATION POSITIVE: LEX LUTHOR.
CONTINUE TO SEARCH FOR GRAVITATIONAL ANOMALIES.
KEEP TRYING TO HACK THE JLA WATCHTOWER COMPUTER.
MY COUNTERPART ALMOST ESCAPED THIS MORNING. RE-ENCRYPT THE LOCKS; WE NEED HIM IN THERE FOR ANOTHER 48 HOURS.
ALSO I NEED HARD COPY: EVERYTHING WE'VE GOT ON THE AIRCRAFT THAT REVERSED OVER THIS MORNING.
OH... AND DIVERT FUNDING FROM OUR ARMAMENTS DIVISION TO... LET'S MAKE IT "GREENPEACE" THIS TIME.
AND ALL OF OUR EMPLOYEES COULD DO WITH A RAISE 200%? THREE.

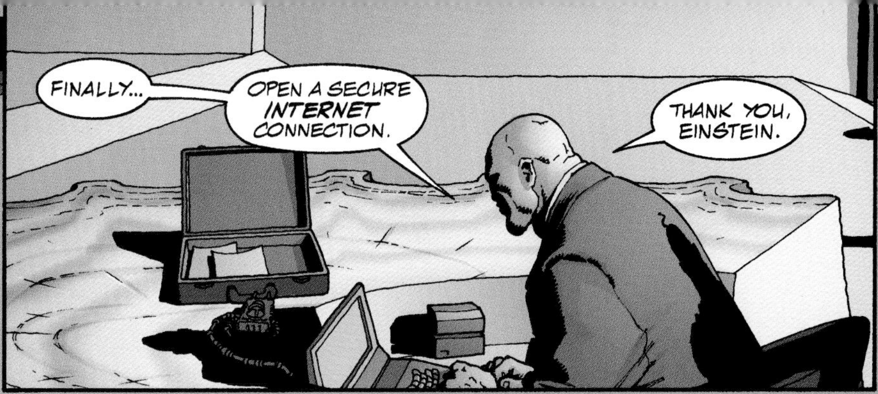
FINALLY...
OPEN A SECURE INTERNET CONNECTION.
THANK YOU, EINSTEIN.

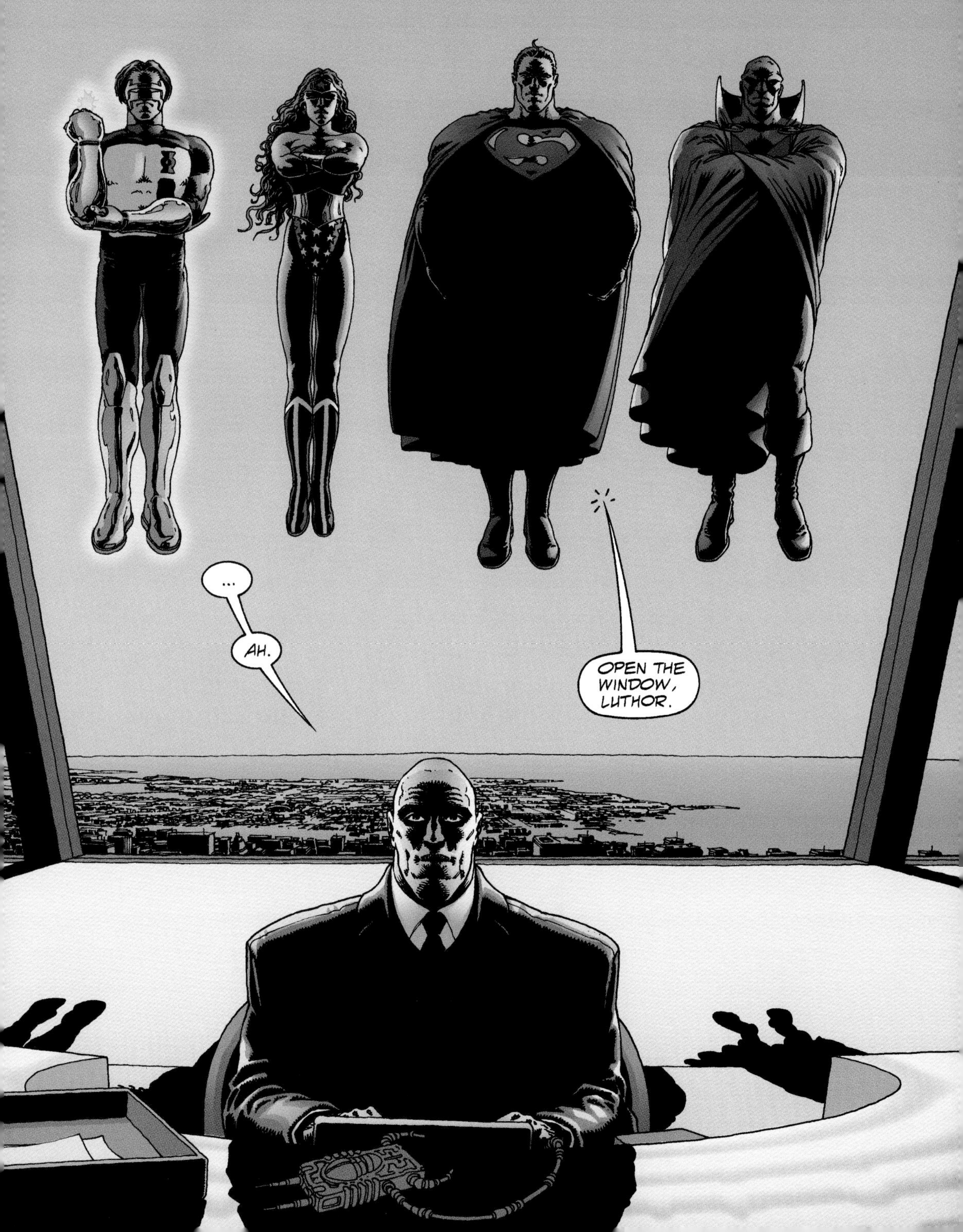
...
AH.
OPEN THE WINDOW, LUTHOR.

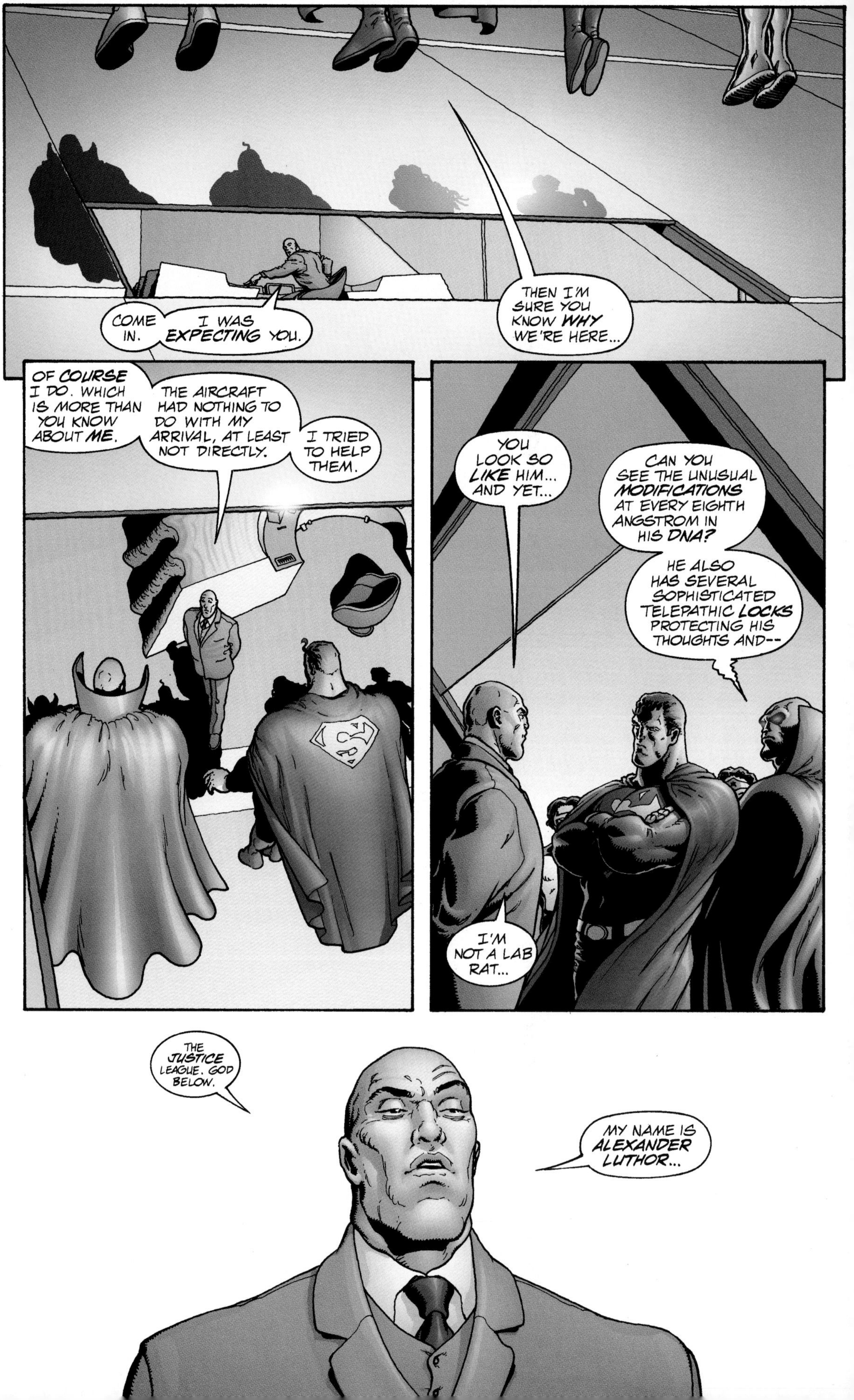
COME IN.
I WAS EXPECTING YOU.
THEN I'M SURE YOU KNOW WHY WE'RE HERE...
OF COURSE I DO. WHICH IS MORE THAN YOU KNOW ABOUT ME.
THE AIRCRAFT HAD NOTHING TO DO WITH MY ARRIVAL, AT LEAST NOT DIRECTLY.
I TRIED TO HELP THEM.
YOU LOOK SO LIKE HIM... AND YET...
CAN YOU SEE THE UNUSUAL MODIFICATIONS AT EVERY EIGHTH ANGSTROM IN HIS DNA?
HE ALSO HAS SEVERAL SOPHISTICATED TELEPATHIC LOCKS PROTECTING HIS THOUGHTS AND--
I'M NOT A LAB RAT...
THE JUSTICE LEAGUE. GOD BELOW.
MY NAME IS ALEXANDER LUTHOR...

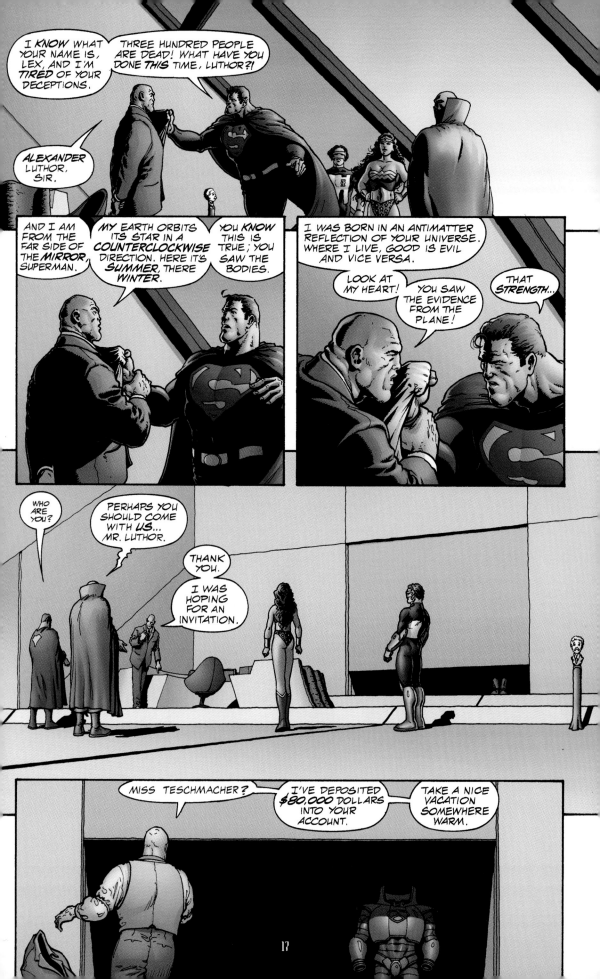

I *KNOW* WHAT YOUR NAME IS, LEX, AND I'M *TIRED* OF YOUR DECEPTIONS.

THREE HUNDRED PEOPLE ARE DEAD! WHAT HAVE YOU DONE *THIS* TIME, LUTHOR?!

ALEXANDER LUTHOR, SIR.

AND I AM FROM THE FAR SIDE OF THE *MIRROR*, SUPERMAN.

MY EARTH ORBITS ITS STAR IN A *COUNTERCLOCKWISE* DIRECTION. HERE IT'S *SUMMER*, THERE *WINTER*.

YOU *KNOW* THIS IS TRUE; YOU SAW THE BODIES.

I WAS BORN IN AN ANTIMATTER REFLECTION OF YOUR UNIVERSE. WHERE I LIVE, GOOD IS EVIL AND VICE VERSA.

LOOK AT MY HEART!

YOU SAW THE EVIDENCE FROM THE PLANE!

THAT *STRENGTH*...

WHO ARE YOU?

PERHAPS YOU SHOULD COME WITH *US*... MR. LUTHOR.

THANK YOU.

I WAS HOPING FOR AN INVITATION.

MISS TESCHMACHER?

I'VE DEPOSITED $80,000 DOLLARS INTO YOUR ACCOUNT.

TAKE A NICE VACATION SOMEWHERE WARM.

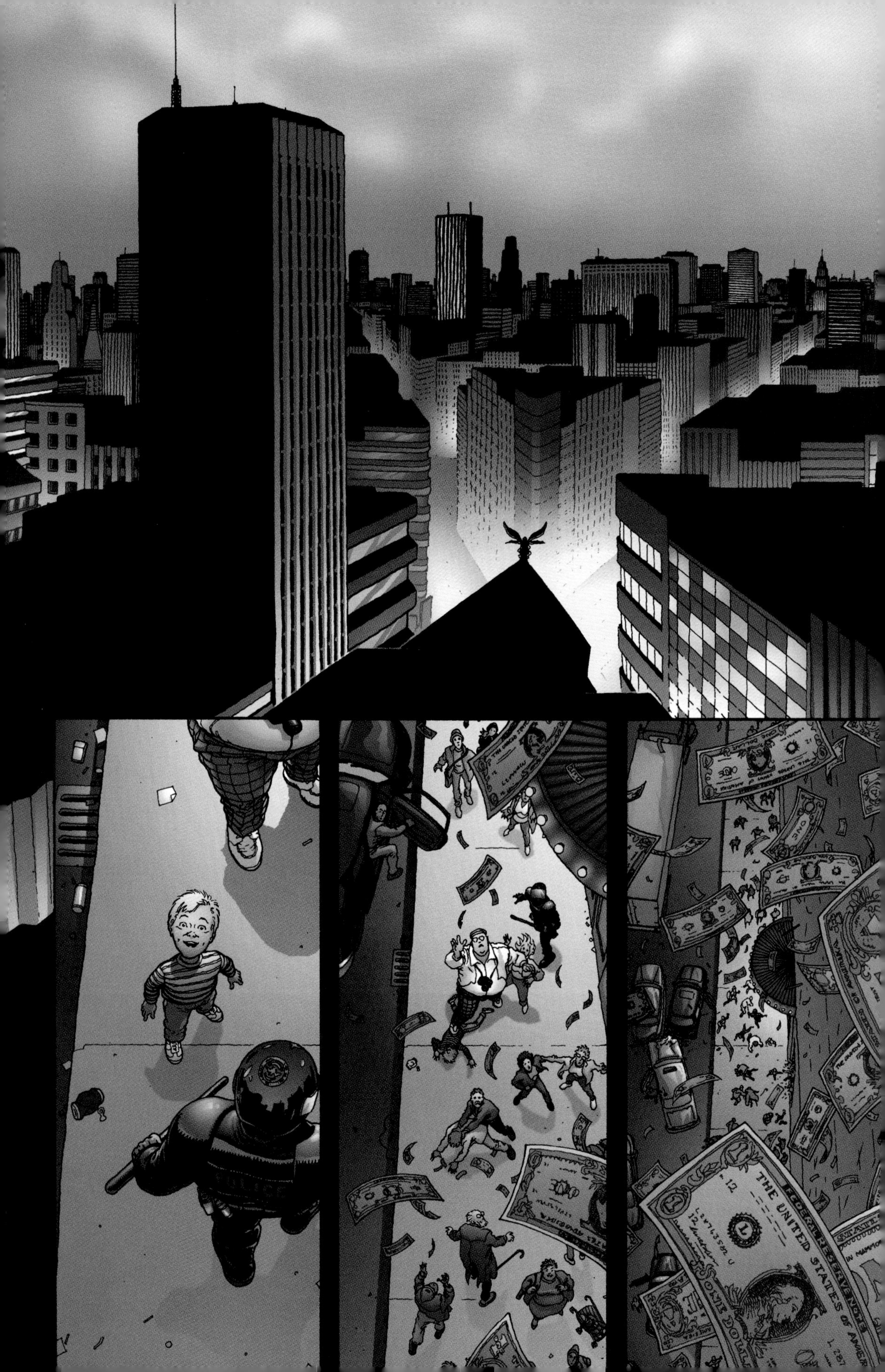
POLICE
THE UNITED STATES

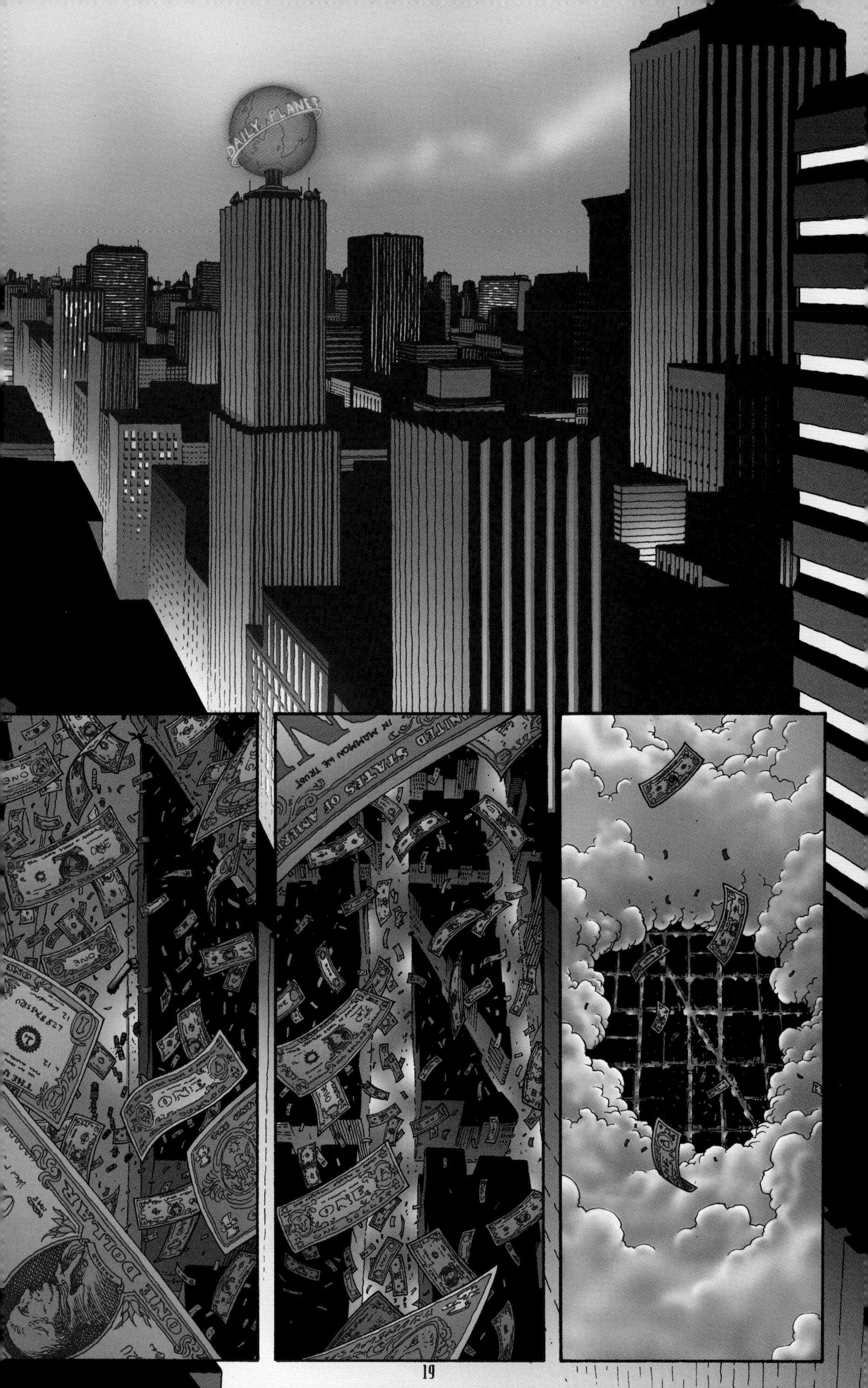
DAILY PLANET
IN MAMMON WE TRUST

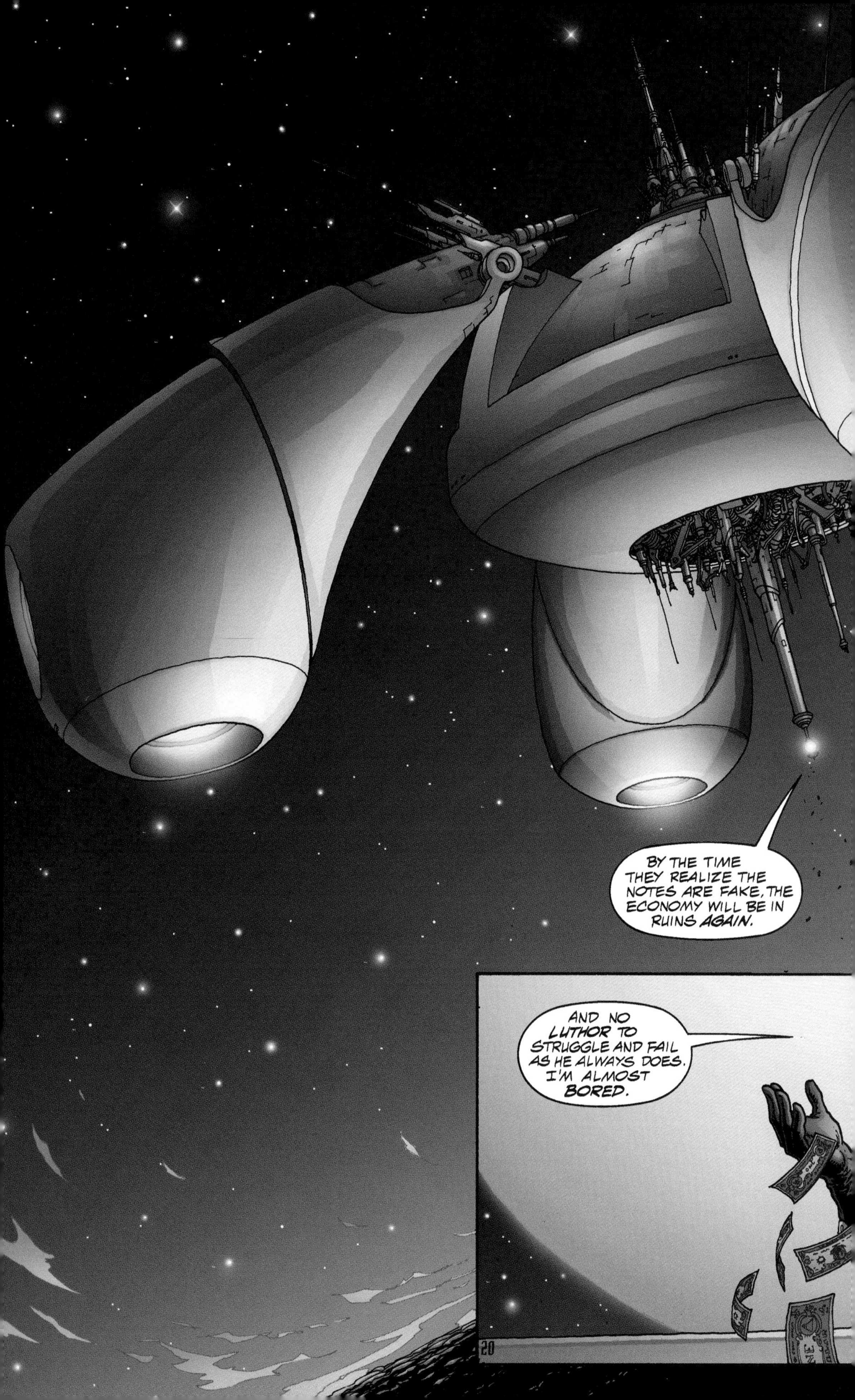
BY THE TIME THEY REALIZE THE NOTES ARE FAKE, THE ECONOMY WILL BE IN RUINS *AGAIN*.
AND NO *LUTHOR* TO STRUGGLE AND FAIL AS HE ALWAYS DOES. I'M ALMOST *BORED*.

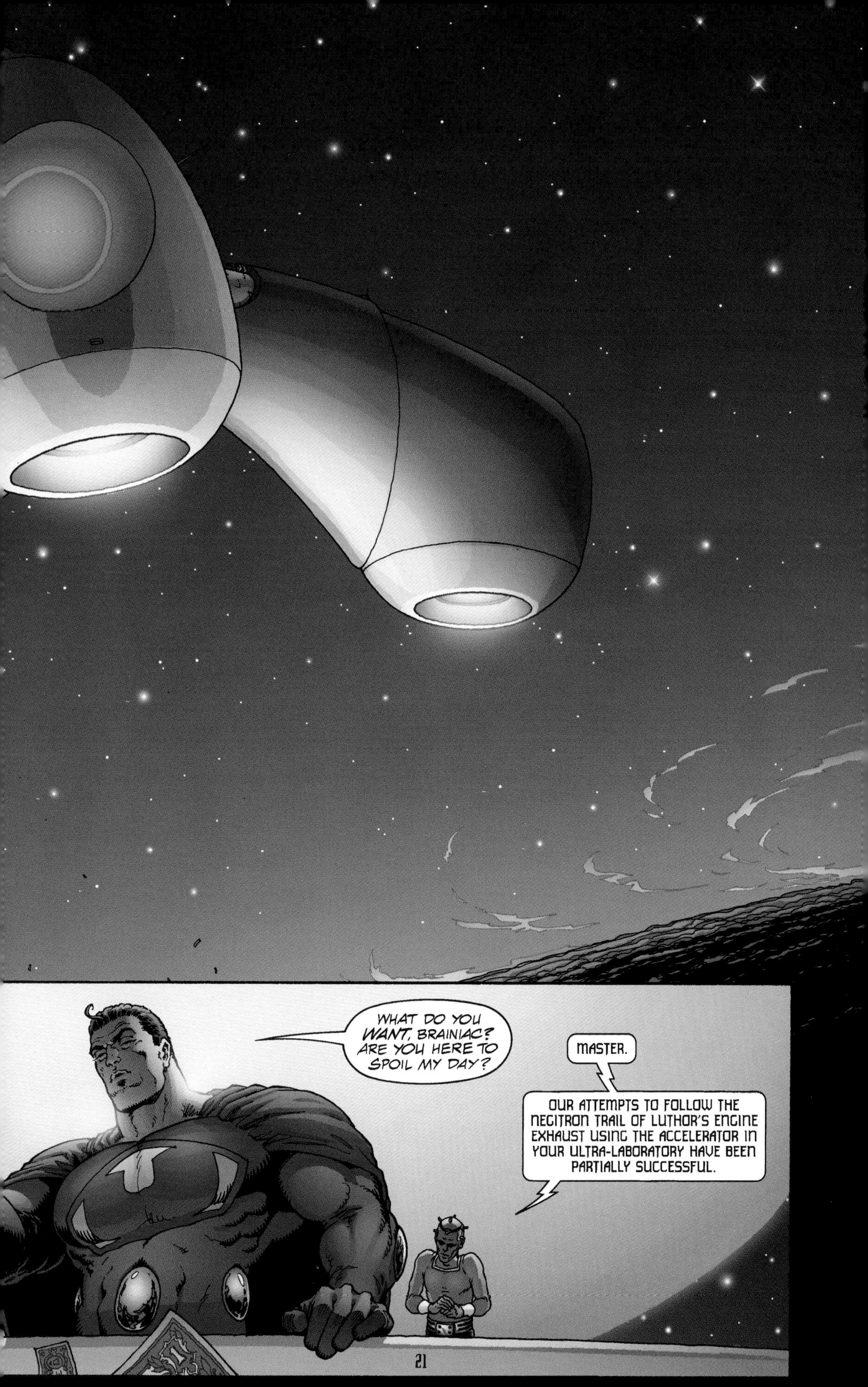

WHAT DO YOU WANT, BRAINIAC? ARE YOU HERE TO SPOIL MY DAY?
MASTER.
OUR ATTEMPTS TO FOLLOW THE NEGITRON TRAIL OF LUTHOR'S ENGINE EXHAUST USING THE ACCELERATOR IN YOUR ULTRA-LABORATORY HAVE BEEN PARTIALLY SUCCESSFUL.

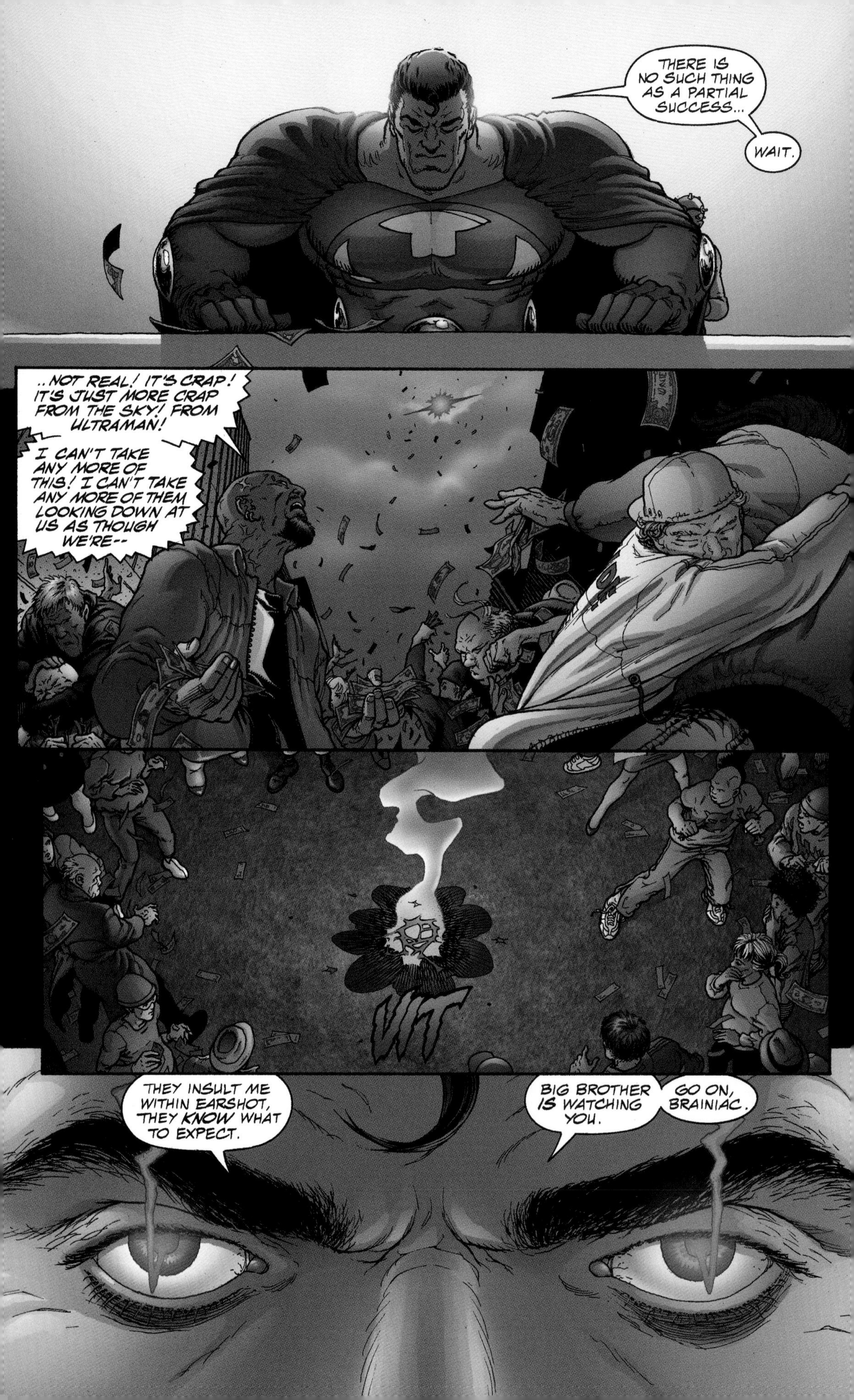
THERE IS NO SUCH THING AS A PARTIAL SUCCESS...
WAIT.
..NOT REAL! IT'S CRAP! IT'S JUST MORE CRAP FROM THE SKY! FROM ULTRAMAN!
I CAN'T TAKE ANY MORE OF THIS! I CAN'T TAKE ANY MORE OF THEM LOOKING DOWN AT US AS THOUGH WE'RE--
VIT
THEY INSULT ME WITHIN EARSHOT, THEY KNOW WHAT TO EXPECT.
BIG BROTHER IS WATCHING YOU.
GO ON, BRAINIAC.

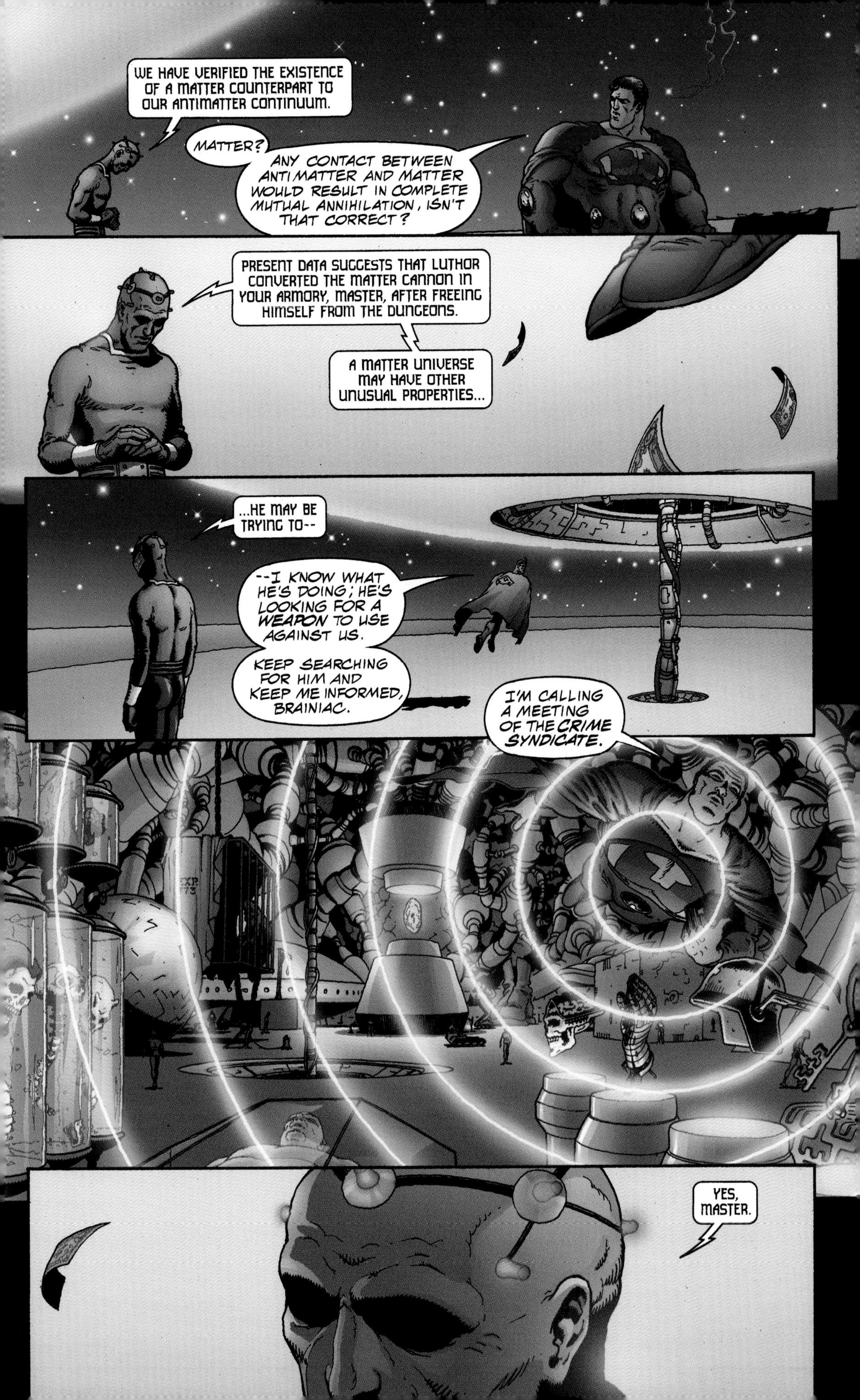
WE HAVE VERIFIED THE EXISTENCE OF A MATTER COUNTERPART TO OUR ANTIMATTER CONTINUUM.
MATTER?
ANY CONTACT BETWEEN ANTIMATTER AND MATTER WOULD RESULT IN COMPLETE MUTUAL ANNIHILATION, ISN'T THAT CORRECT?
PRESENT DATA SUGGESTS THAT LUTHOR CONVERTED THE MATTER CANNON IN YOUR ARMORY, MASTER, AFTER FREEING HIMSELF FROM THE DUNGEONS.
A MATTER UNIVERSE MAY HAVE OTHER UNUSUAL PROPERTIES...
...HE MAY BE TRYING TO--
--I KNOW WHAT HE'S DOING; HE'S LOOKING FOR A WEAPON TO USE AGAINST US.
KEEP SEARCHING FOR HIM AND KEEP ME INFORMED, BRAINIAC.
I'M CALLING A MEETING OF THE CRIME SYNDICATE.
YES, MASTER.

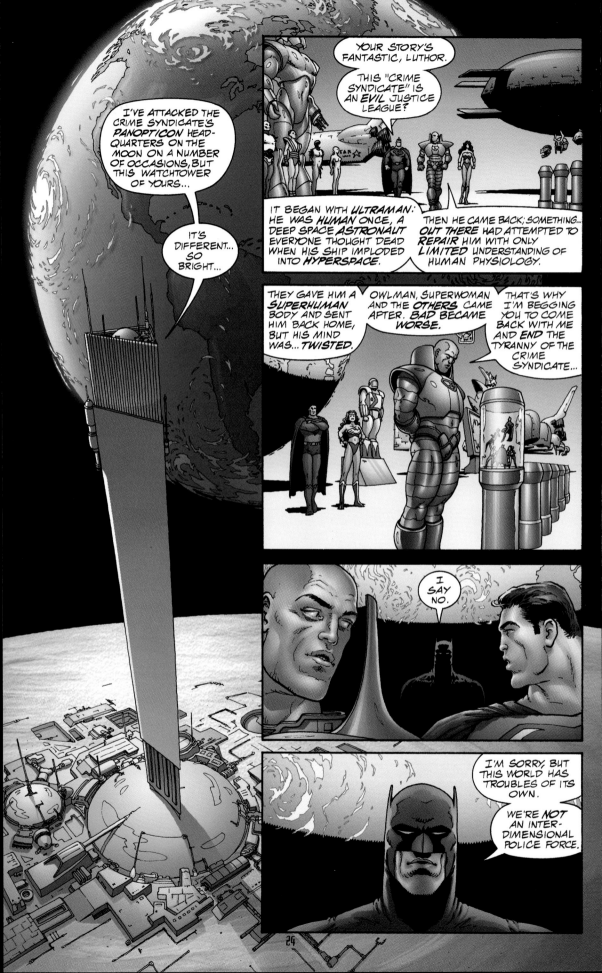

I'VE ATTACKED THE CRIME SYNDICATE'S *PANOPTICON* HEAD-QUARTERS ON THE MOON ON A NUMBER OF OCCASIONS, BUT THIS WATCHTOWER OF YOURS...

IT'S DIFFERENT... SO BRIGHT...

YOUR STORY'S FANTASTIC, LUTHOR.

THIS "CRIME SYNDICATE" IS AN *EVIL* JUSTICE LEAGUE?

IT BEGAN WITH *ULTRAMAN*: HE WAS *HUMAN* ONCE, A DEEP SPACE *ASTRONAUT* EVERYONE THOUGHT DEAD WHEN HIS SHIP IMPLODED INTO *HYPERSPACE*.

THEN HE CAME BACK; SOMETHING... *OUT THERE* HAD ATTEMPTED TO *REPAIR* HIM WITH ONLY *LIMITED* UNDERSTANDING OF HUMAN PHYSIOLOGY.

THEY GAVE HIM A *SUPERHUMAN* BODY AND SENT HIM BACK HOME, BUT HIS MIND WAS... *TWISTED*.

OWLMAN, SUPERWOMAN AND THE *OTHERS* CAME AFTER. *BAD BECAME WORSE*.

THAT'S WHY I'M BEGGING YOU TO COME BACK WITH ME AND *END* THE TYRANNY OF THE CRIME SYNDICATE...

I SAY NO.

I'M SORRY, BUT THIS WORLD HAS TROUBLES OF ITS OWN.

WE'RE *NOT* AN INTER-DIMENSIONAL POLICE FORCE.

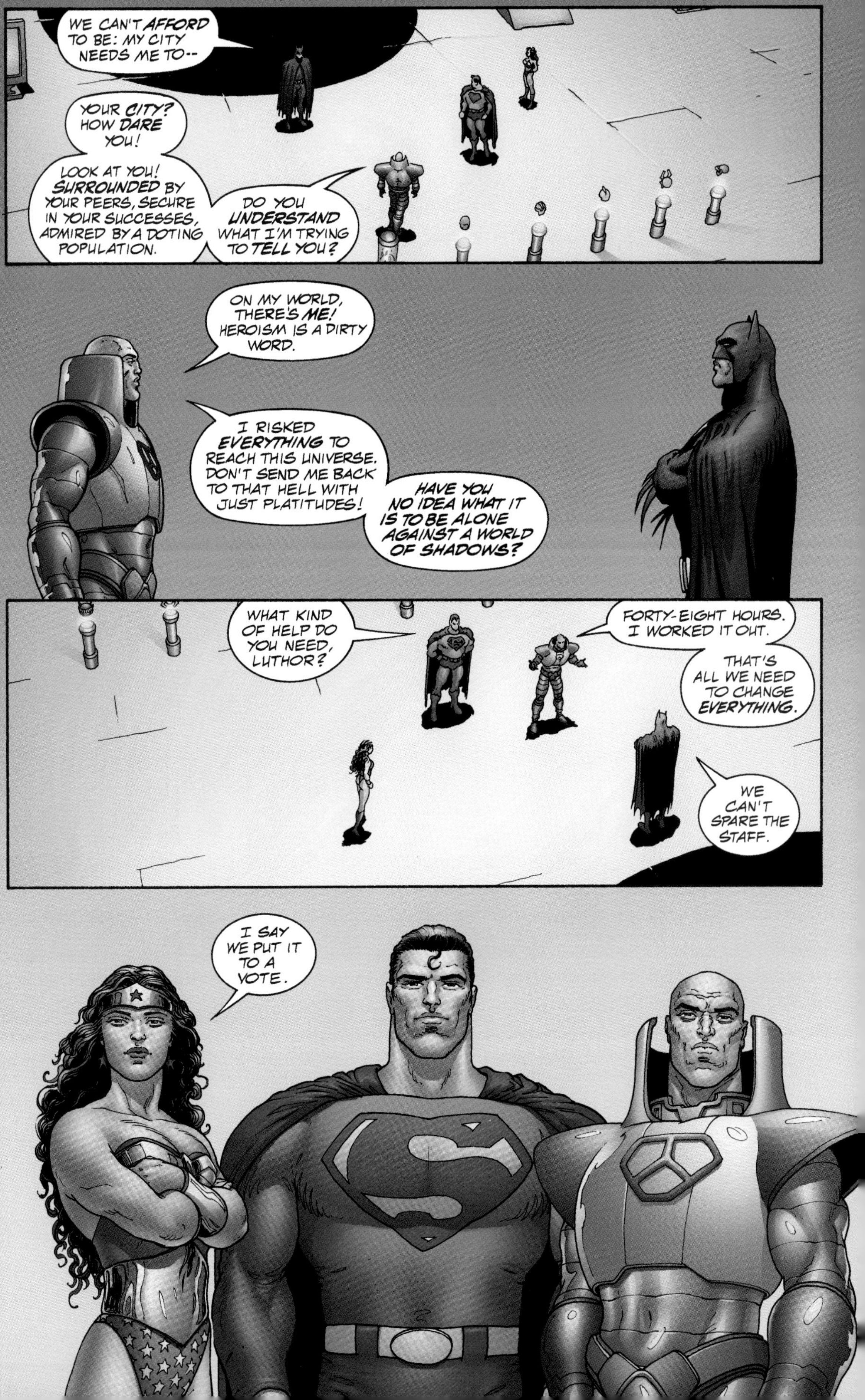
WE CAN'T AFFORD TO BE: MY CITY NEEDS ME TO--
YOUR CITY? HOW DARE YOU!
LOOK AT YOU! SURROUNDED BY YOUR PEERS, SECURE IN YOUR SUCCESSES, ADMIRED BY A DOTING POPULATION.
DO YOU UNDERSTAND WHAT I'M TRYING TO TELL YOU?
ON MY WORLD, THERE'S ME! HEROISM IS A DIRTY WORD.
I RISKED EVERYTHING TO REACH THIS UNIVERSE. DON'T SEND ME BACK TO THAT HELL WITH JUST PLATITUDES!
HAVE YOU NO IDEA WHAT IT IS TO BE ALONE AGAINST A WORLD OF SHADOWS?
WHAT KIND OF HELP DO YOU NEED, LUTHOR?
FORTY-EIGHT HOURS. I WORKED IT OUT.
THAT'S ALL WE NEED TO CHANGE EVERYTHING.
WE CAN'T SPARE THE STAFF.
I SAY WE PUT IT TO A VOTE.

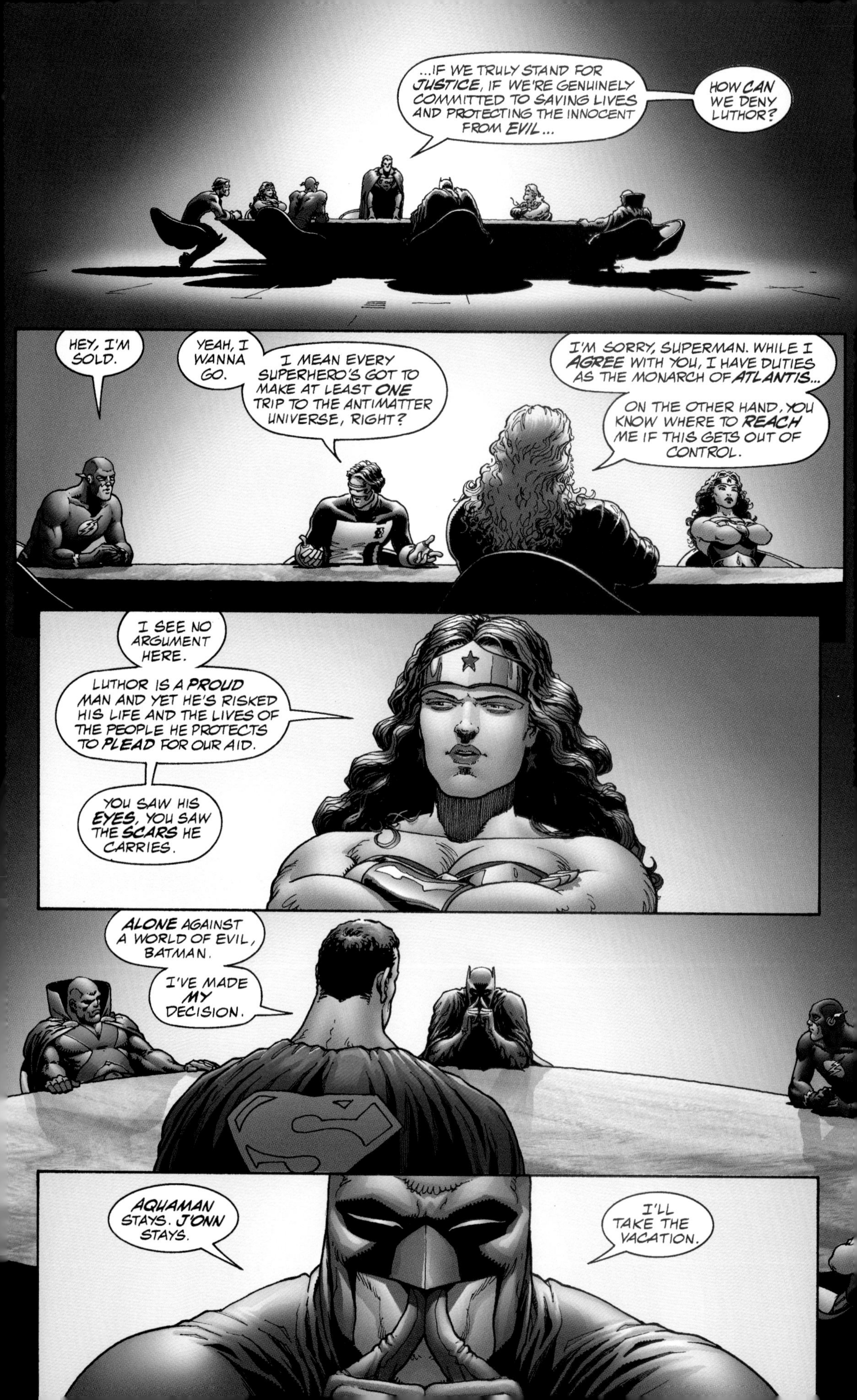
...IF WE TRULY STAND FOR JUSTICE, IF WE'RE GENUINELY COMMITTED TO SAVING LIVES AND PROTECTING THE INNOCENT FROM EVIL...
HOW CAN WE DENY LUTHOR?
HEY, I'M SOLD.
YEAH, I WANNA GO.
I MEAN EVERY SUPERHERO'S GOT TO MAKE AT LEAST ONE TRIP TO THE ANTIMATTER UNIVERSE, RIGHT?
I'M SORRY, SUPERMAN. WHILE I AGREE WITH YOU, I HAVE DUTIES AS THE MONARCH OF ATLANTIS...
ON THE OTHER HAND, YOU KNOW WHERE TO REACH ME IF THIS GETS OUT OF CONTROL.
I SEE NO ARGUMENT HERE.
LUTHOR IS A PROUD MAN AND YET HE'S RISKED HIS LIFE AND THE LIVES OF THE PEOPLE HE PROTECTS TO PLEAD FOR OUR AID.
YOU SAW HIS EYES, YOU SAW THE SCARS HE CARRIES.
ALONE AGAINST A WORLD OF EVIL, BATMAN.
I'VE MADE MY DECISION.
AQUAMAN STAYS. J'ONN STAYS.
I'LL TAKE THE VACATION.

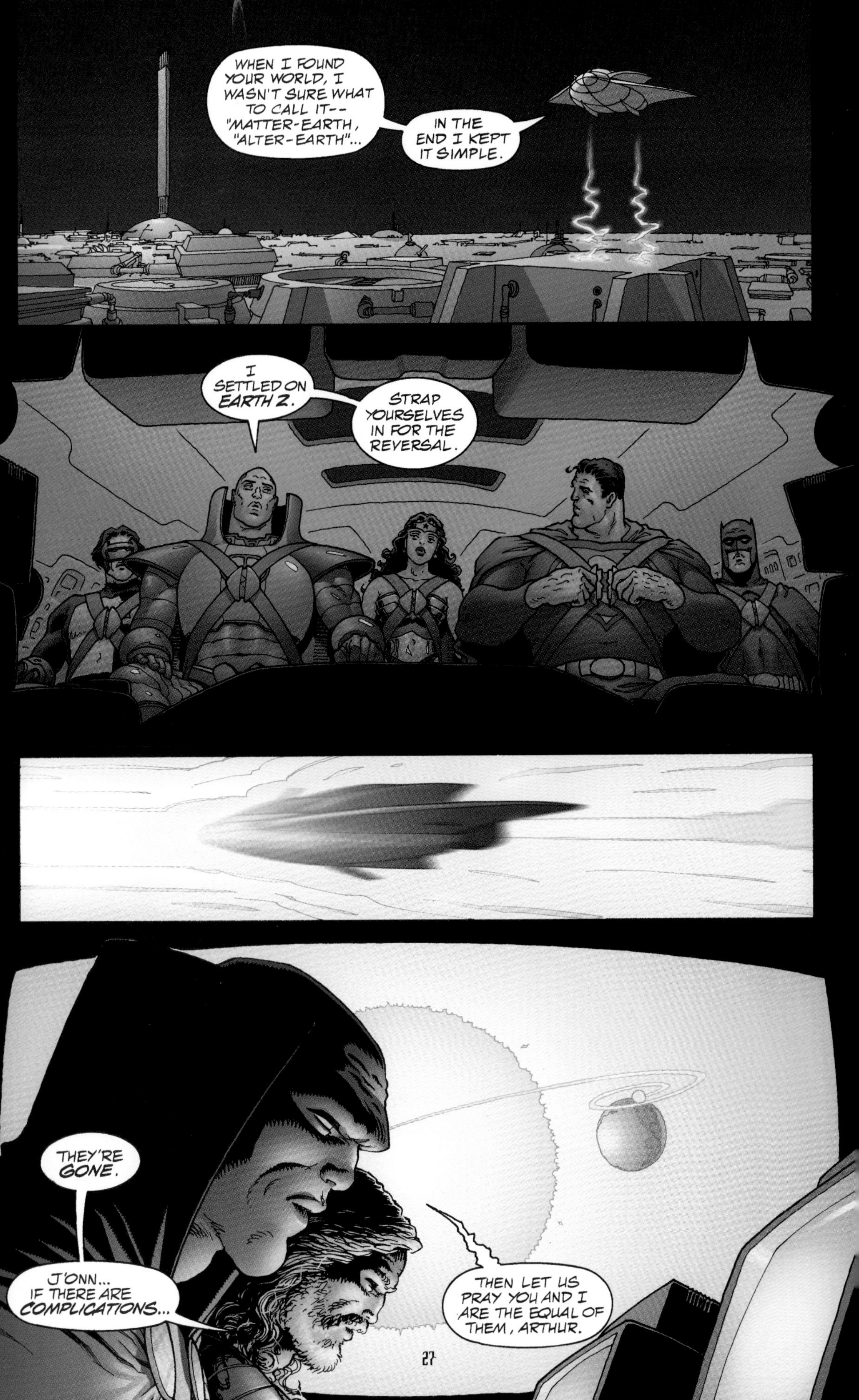
WHEN I FOUND YOUR WORLD, I WASN'T SURE WHAT TO CALL IT-- "MATTER-EARTH," "ALTER-EARTH"...
IN THE END I KEPT IT SIMPLE.
I SETTLED ON EARTH 2.
STRAP YOURSELVES IN FOR THE REVERSAL.
THEY'RE GONE.
J'ONN... IF THERE ARE COMPLICATIONS...
THEN LET US PRAY YOU AND I ARE THE EQUAL OF THEM, ARTHUR.

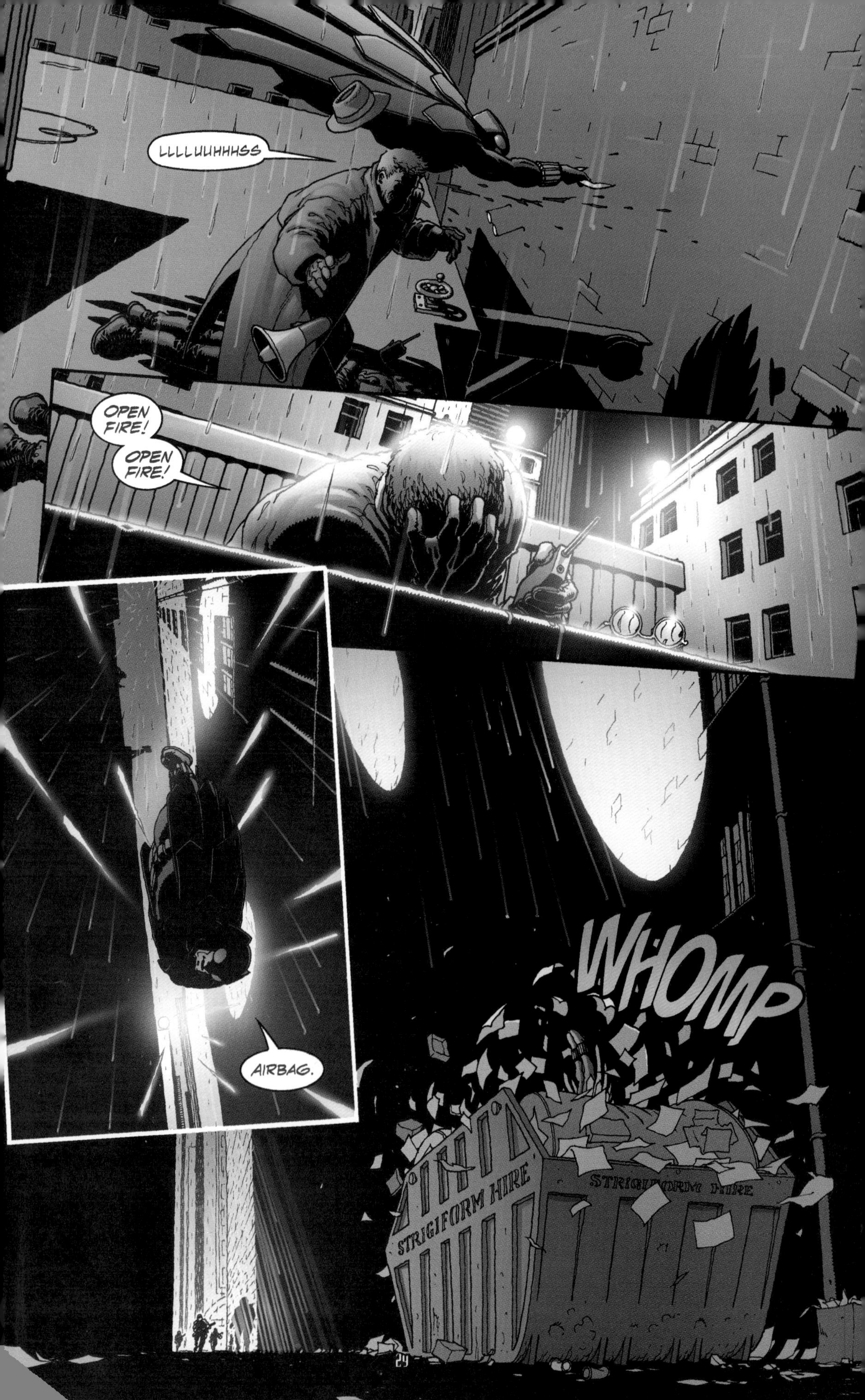
LLLLUUHHHSS
OPEN FIRE!
OPEN FIRE!
AIRBAG.
WHOMP
STRIGIFORM HIRE
STRIGIFORM HIRE

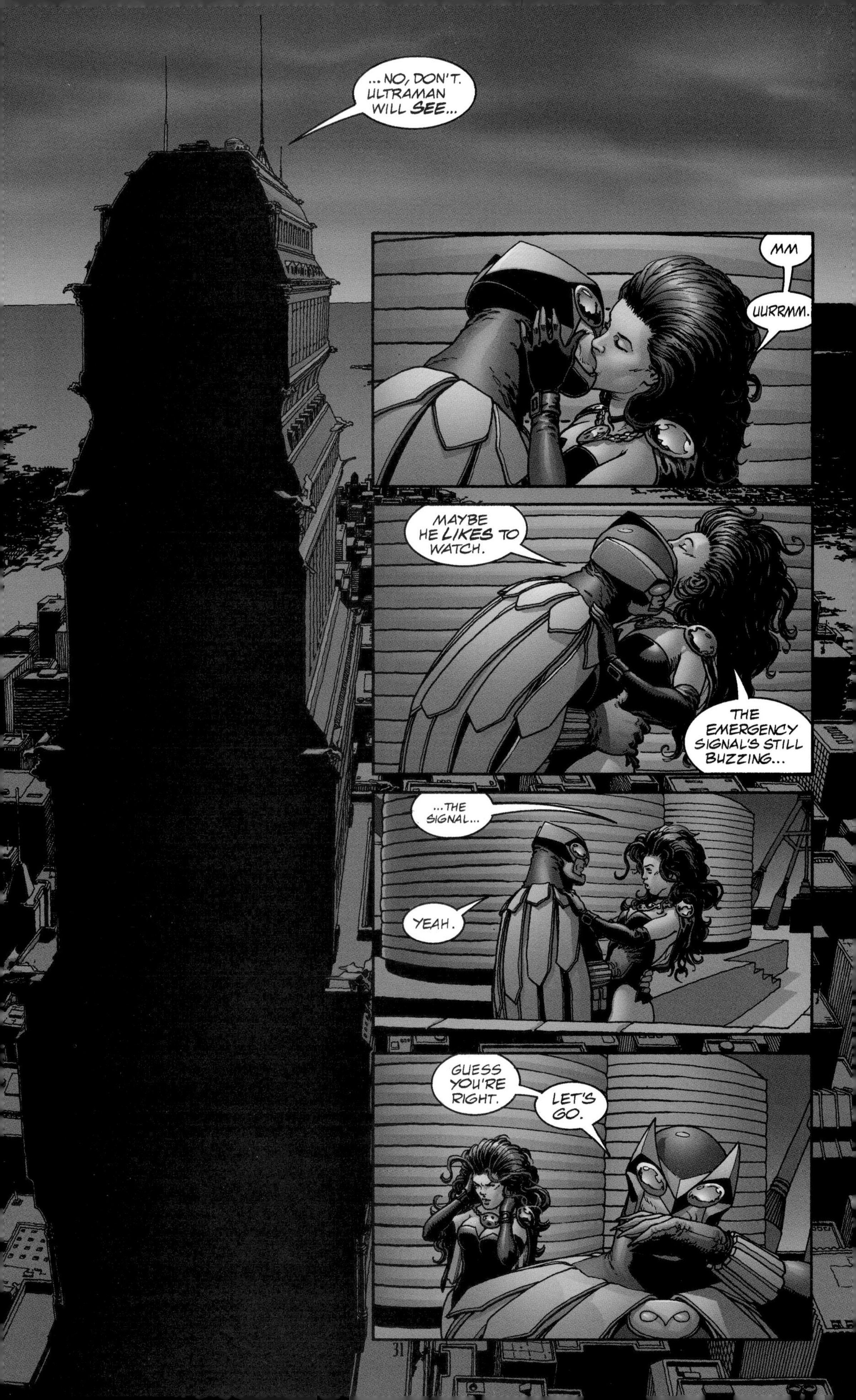
...NO, DON'T. ULTRAMAN WILL SEE...
MM
UURRMM.
MAYBE HE LIKES TO WATCH.
THE EMERGENCY SIGNAL'S STILL BUZZING...
...THE SIGNAL...
YEAH.
GUESS YOU'RE RIGHT.
LET'S GO.

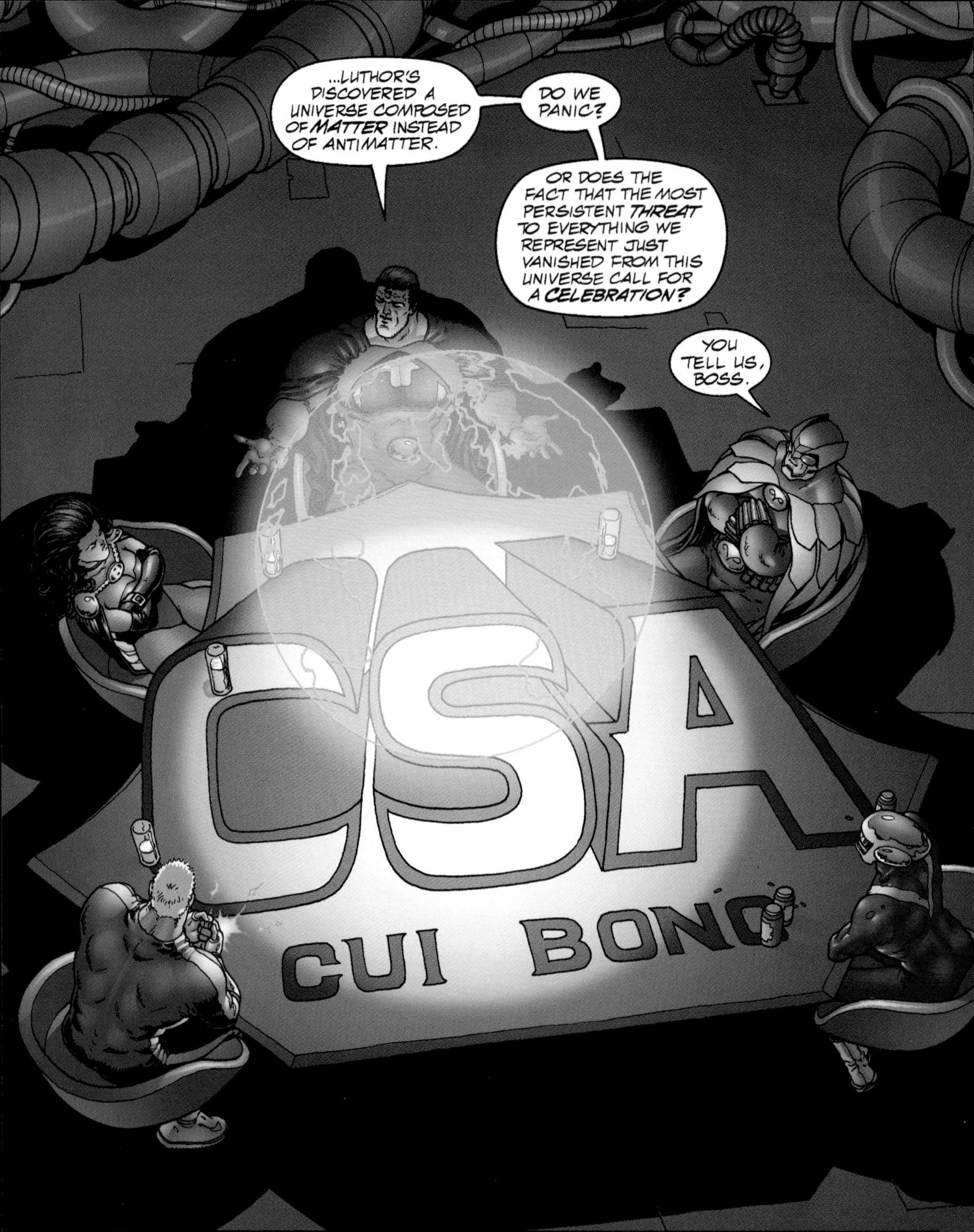

...LUTHOR'S DISCOVERED A UNIVERSE COMPOSED OF MATTER INSTEAD OF ANTIMATTER.
DO WE PANIC?
OR DOES THE FACT THAT THE MOST PERSISTENT THREAT TO EVERYTHING WE REPRESENT JUST VANISHED FROM THIS UNIVERSE CALL FOR A CELEBRATION?
YOU TELL US, BOSS.
CSA
CUI BONO

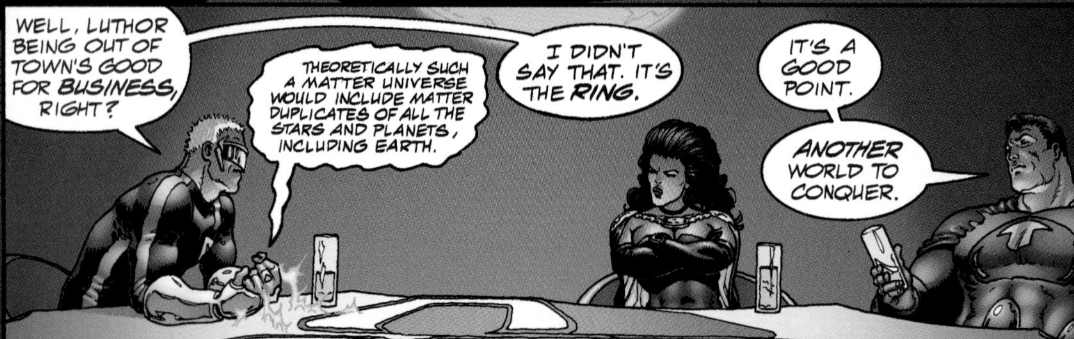

WELL, LUTHOR BEING OUT OF TOWN'S GOOD FOR BUSINESS, RIGHT?
THEORETICALLY SUCH A MATTER UNIVERSE WOULD INCLUDE MATTER DUPLICATES OF ALL THE STARS AND PLANETS, INCLUDING EARTH.
I DIDN'T SAY THAT. IT'S THE RING.
IT'S A GOOD POINT.
ANOTHER WORLD TO CONQUER.

EXACTLY. EXACTLY WHAT I'M SAYING. ULTRAMAN'S *TOTALLY* RIGHT.

WE SHOULD BE THINKING ABOUT HOW WE CAN *EXPLOIT* THIS.

IF LUTHOR WANTS A *CHALLENGE*, HE'LL GET ONE. THINK OF THIS MATTER UNIVERSE AS JUST ONE MORE VULNERABLE *FREIGHTER* LADEN WITH TREASURE.

HOIST THE *JOLLY ROGER* HIGH...

AND PREPARE TO BOARD.

WHAT WAS THAT *PIRATE* DRIVEL?

TALK TO ME. WHAT DOES "MATTER DUPLICATES" OF OURSELVES *IMPLY* TO YOU? IT WAS YOUR TECHNOLOGY LUTHOR *USED* TO ESCAPE...

I'LL SPEAK TO YOU AFTER I SPEAK TO *HER.*

ONE OF THESE DAYS YOU'LL GO TOO FAR, OWLMAN, AND YOU WON'T COME *BACK.*

DOCTOR NOON

WHITE CAT

SPACE MAN

SURE.

UNTIL THEN I HAVE THE *NEGATIVES,* REMEMBER?

ONE DAY.

33

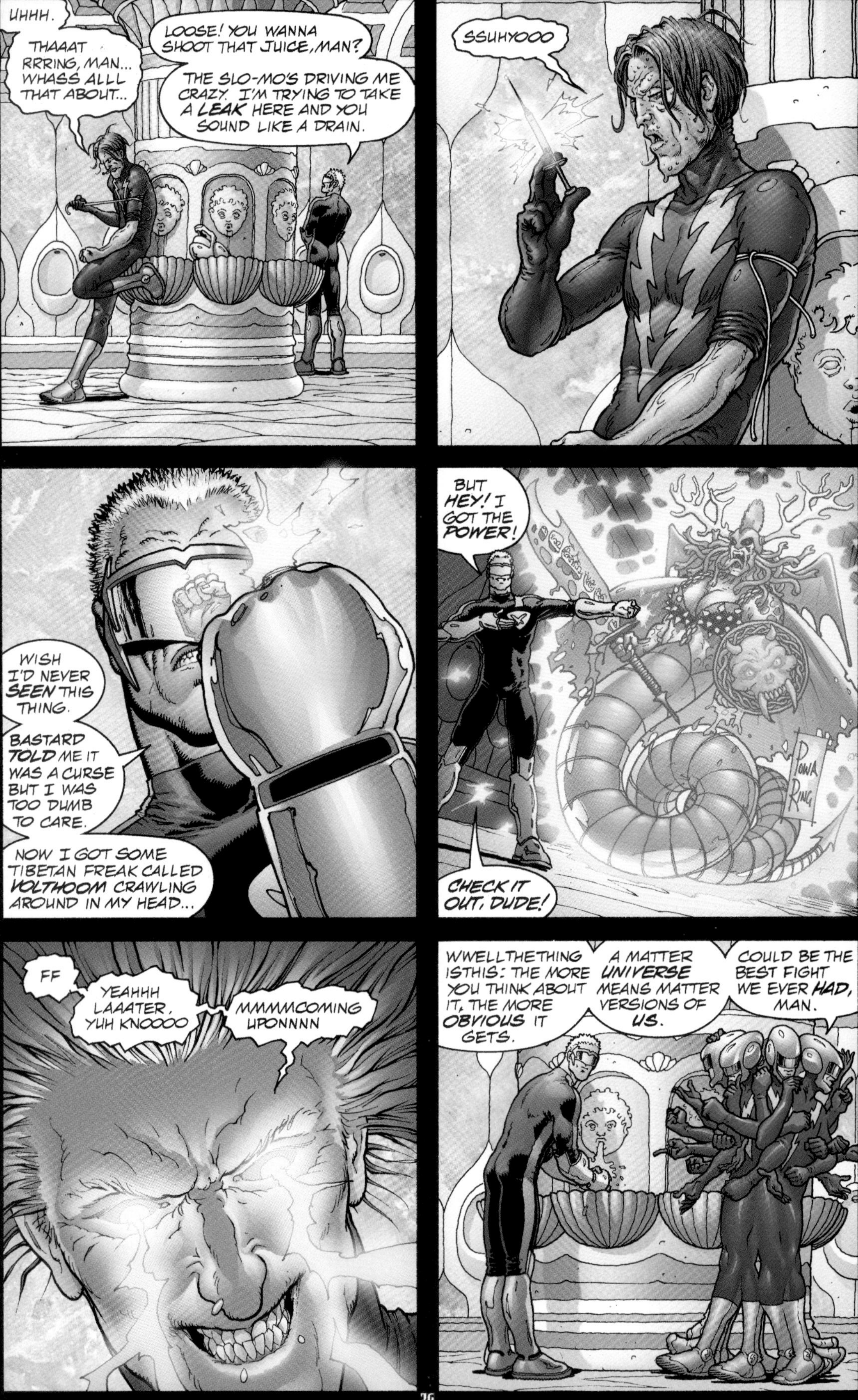
UHHH.
THAAAT RRRING, MAN... WHASS ALLL THAT ABOUT...
LOOSE! YOU WANNA SHOOT THAT JUICE, MAN?
THE SLO-MO'S DRIVING ME CRAZY. I'M TRYING TO TAKE A LEAK HERE AND YOU SOUND LIKE A DRAIN.
SSUHYOOO
WISH I'D NEVER SEEN THIS THING.
BASTARD TOLD ME IT WAS A CURSE BUT I WAS TOO DUMB TO CARE.
NOW I GOT SOME TIBETAN FREAK CALLED VOLTHOOM CRAWLING AROUND IN MY HEAD...
BUT HEY! I GOT THE POWER!
POWA RING
CHECK IT OUT, DUDE!
FF
YEAHHH LAAATER, YUH KNOOOO
MMMMCOMING UPONNNN
WWELLTHETHING ISTHIS: THE MORE YOU THINK ABOUT IT, THE MORE OBVIOUS IT GETS.
A MATTER UNIVERSE MEANS MATTER VERSIONS OF US.
COULD BE THE BEST FIGHT WE EVER HAD, MAN.

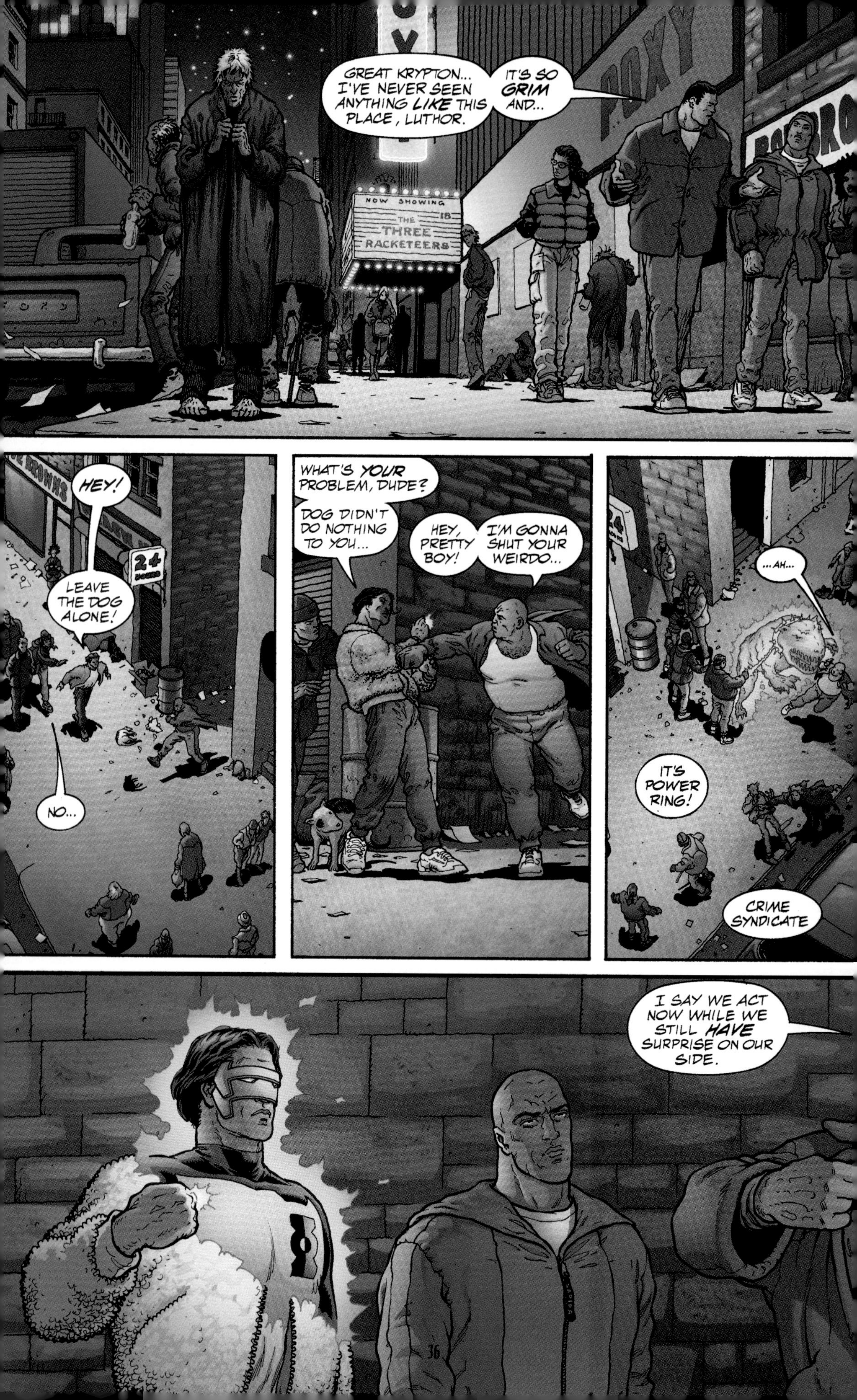

GREAT KRYPTON... I'VE NEVER SEEN ANYTHING *LIKE* THIS PLACE, LUTHOR.
IT'S SO *GRIM* AND...
POXY
NOW SHOWING
THE THREE RACKETEERS
18
HEY!
LEAVE THE DOG ALONE!
NO...
WHAT'S *YOUR* PROBLEM, DUDE?
DOG DIDN'T DO NOTHING TO YOU...
HEY, PRETTY BOY!
I'M GONNA SHUT YOUR WEIRDO...
...AH...
IT'S POWER RING!
CRIME SYNDICATE
I SAY WE ACT NOW WHILE WE STILL *HAVE* SURPRISE ON OUR SIDE.

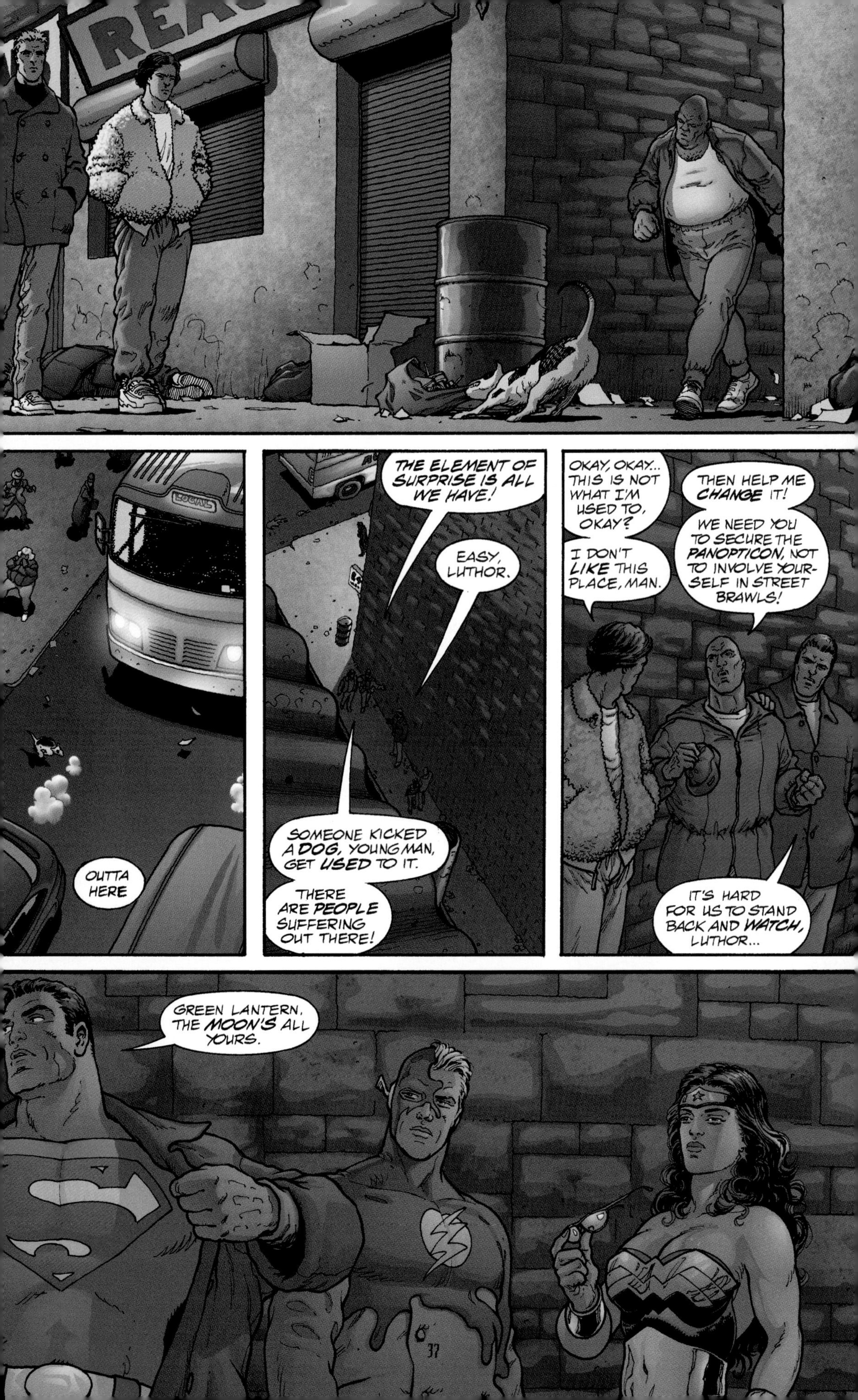

OUTTA HERE
THE ELEMENT OF SURPRISE IS ALL WE HAVE!
EASY, LUTHOR.
SOMEONE KICKED A DOG, YOUNG MAN, GET USED TO IT.
THERE ARE PEOPLE SUFFERING OUT THERE!
OKAY, OKAY... THIS IS NOT WHAT I'M USED TO, OKAY?
I DON'T LIKE THIS PLACE, MAN.
THEN HELP ME CHANGE IT!
WE NEED YOU TO SECURE THE PANOPTICON, NOT TO INVOLVE YOURSELF IN STREET BRAWLS!
IT'S HARD FOR US TO STAND BACK AND WATCH, LUTHOR...
GREEN LANTERN, THE MOON'S ALL YOURS.

WE CAN STILL GET HIM.

TOM, YOU'RE ON YOUR *OWN.*

YOU SHOULD GO HOME. YOU DON'T LOOK SO GOOD.

...GUYS ARE *SCARED,* TOM. THESE MEN AND WOMEN, HAVE *FAMILIES.*

THE BASTARD'S GOT NAMES AND ADDRESSES ON THAT DISK.

WE CAN STILL STOP HIM...

COMMISSIONER WAYNE?

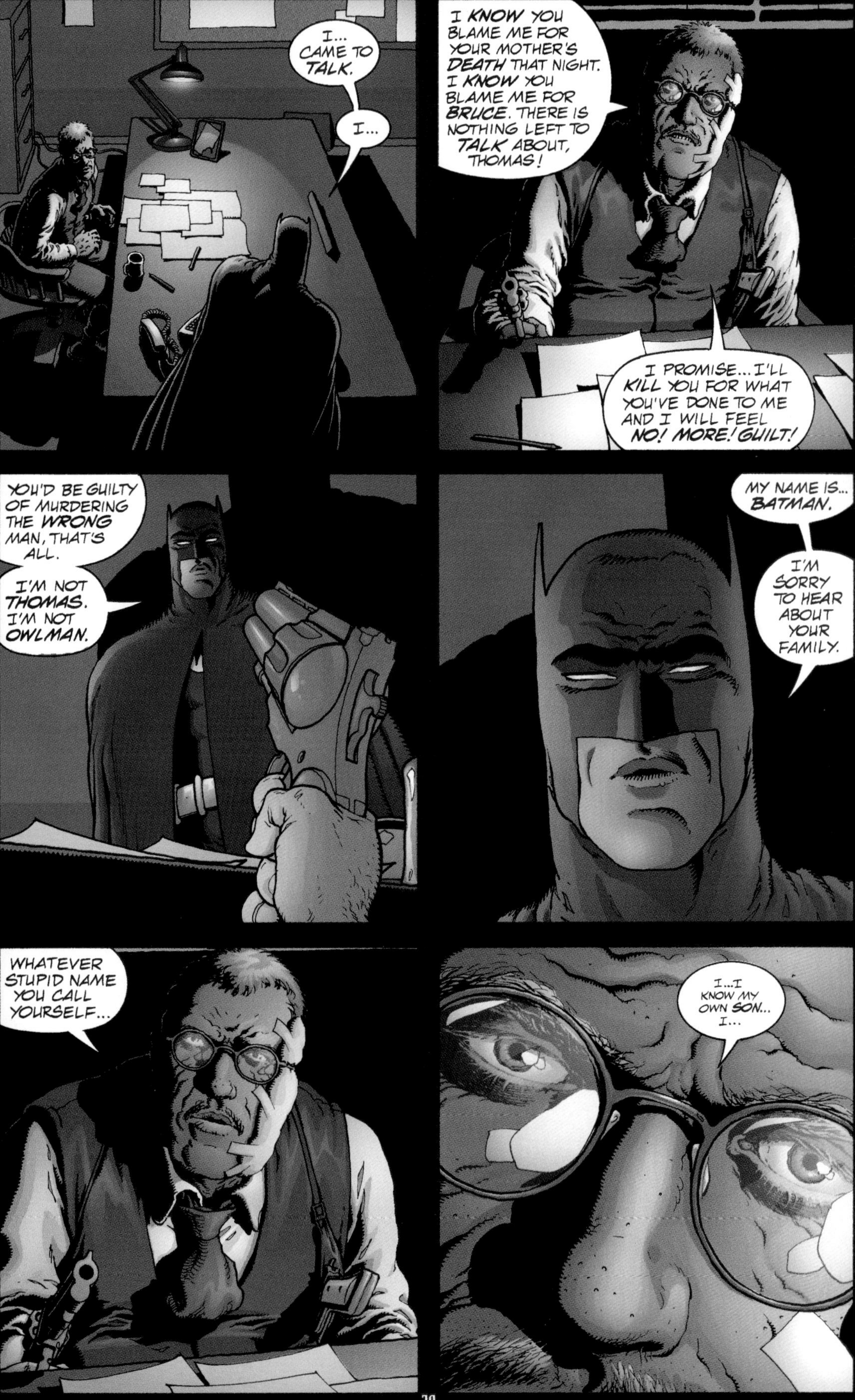
I... CAME TO TALK.
I...
I KNOW YOU BLAME ME FOR YOUR MOTHER'S DEATH THAT NIGHT. I KNOW YOU BLAME ME FOR BRUCE. THERE IS NOTHING LEFT TO TALK ABOUT, THOMAS!
I PROMISE... I'LL KILL YOU FOR WHAT YOU'VE DONE TO ME AND I WILL FEEL NO! MORE! GUILT!
YOU'D BE GUILTY OF MURDERING THE WRONG MAN, THAT'S ALL.
I'M NOT THOMAS. I'M NOT OWLMAN.
MY NAME IS... BATMAN.
I'M SORRY TO HEAR ABOUT YOUR FAMILY.
WHATEVER STUPID NAME YOU CALL YOURSELF...
I...I KNOW MY OWN SON... I...

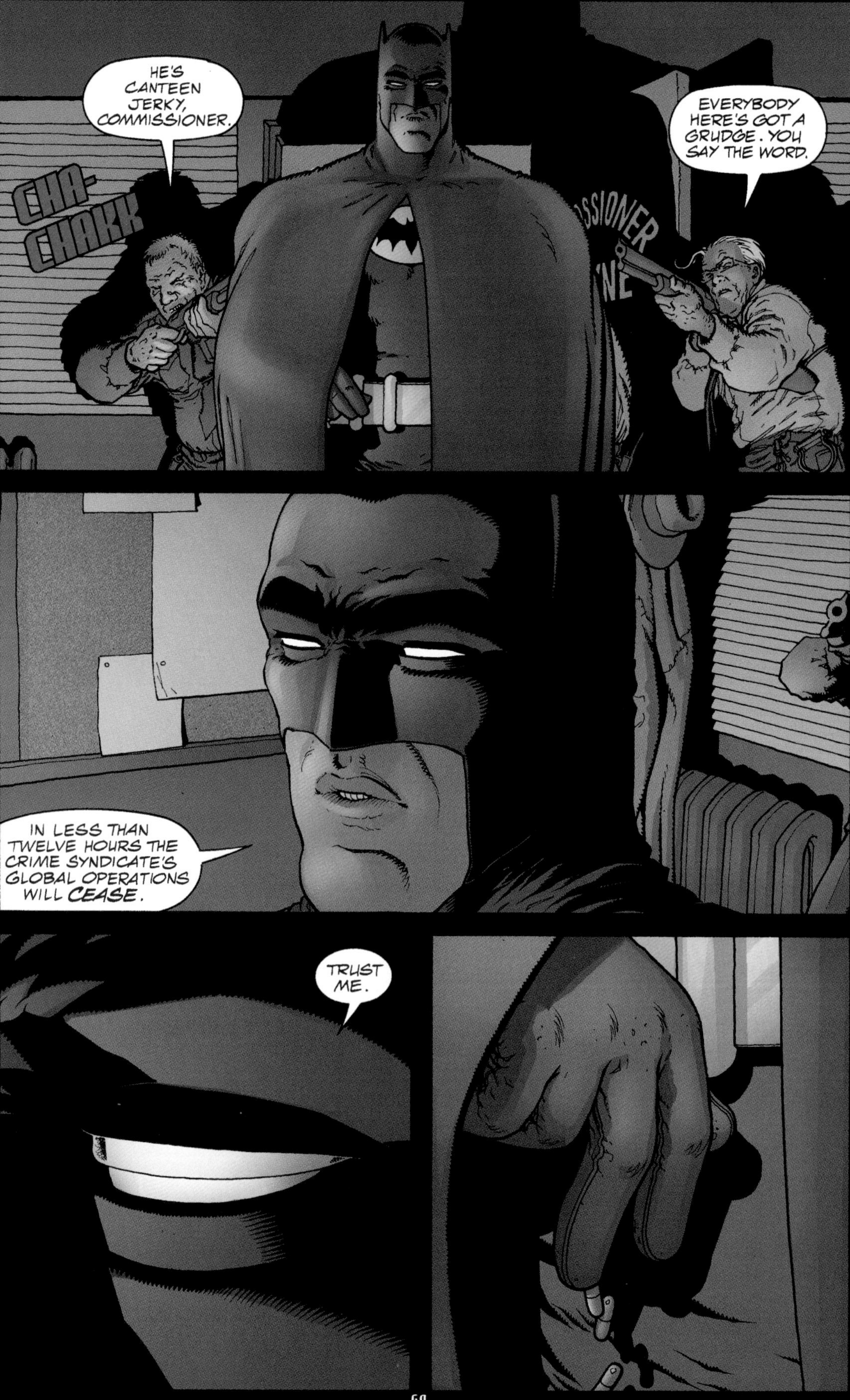

HE'S CANTEEN JERKY, COMMISSIONER.
CHA-CHAKK
EVERYBODY HERE'S GOT A GRUDGE. YOU SAY THE WORD.
IN LESS THAN TWELVE HOURS THE CRIME SYNDICATE'S GLOBAL OPERATIONS WILL CEASE.
TRUST ME.

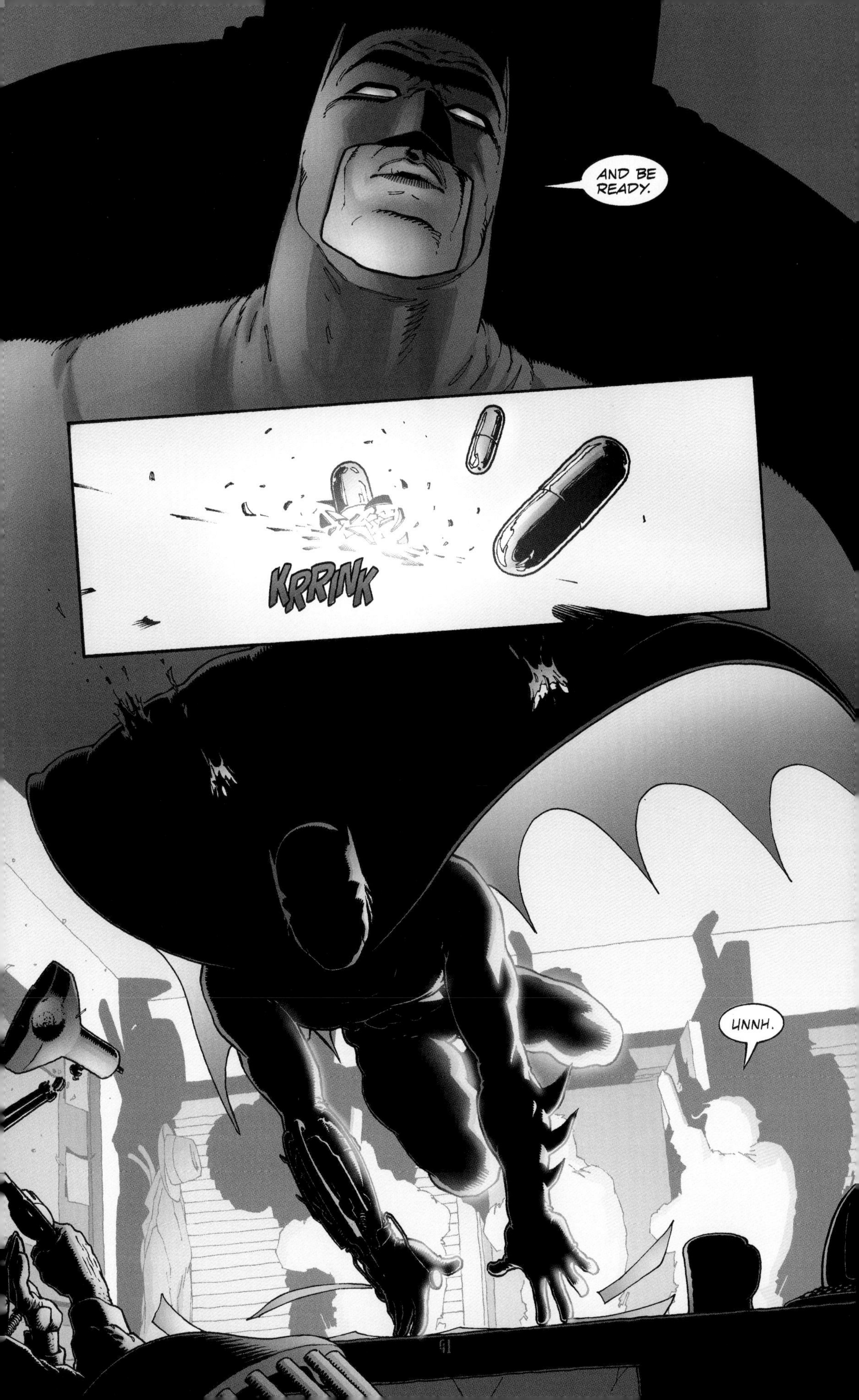
AND BE READY.
KRRINK
UNNH.

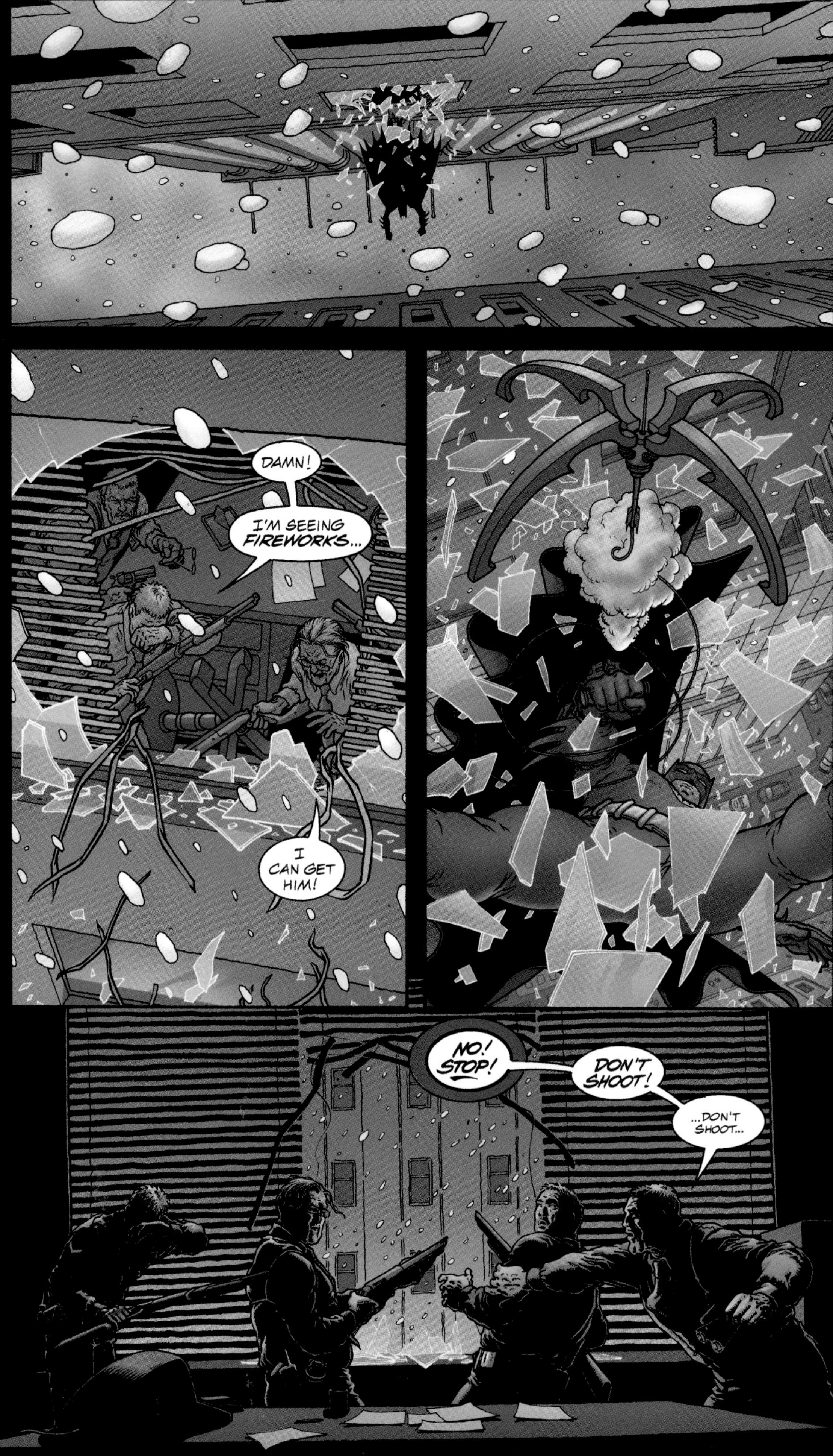
DAMN!
I'M SEEING FIREWORKS...
I CAN GET HIM!
NO! STOP!
DON'T SHOOT!
...DON'T SHOOT...

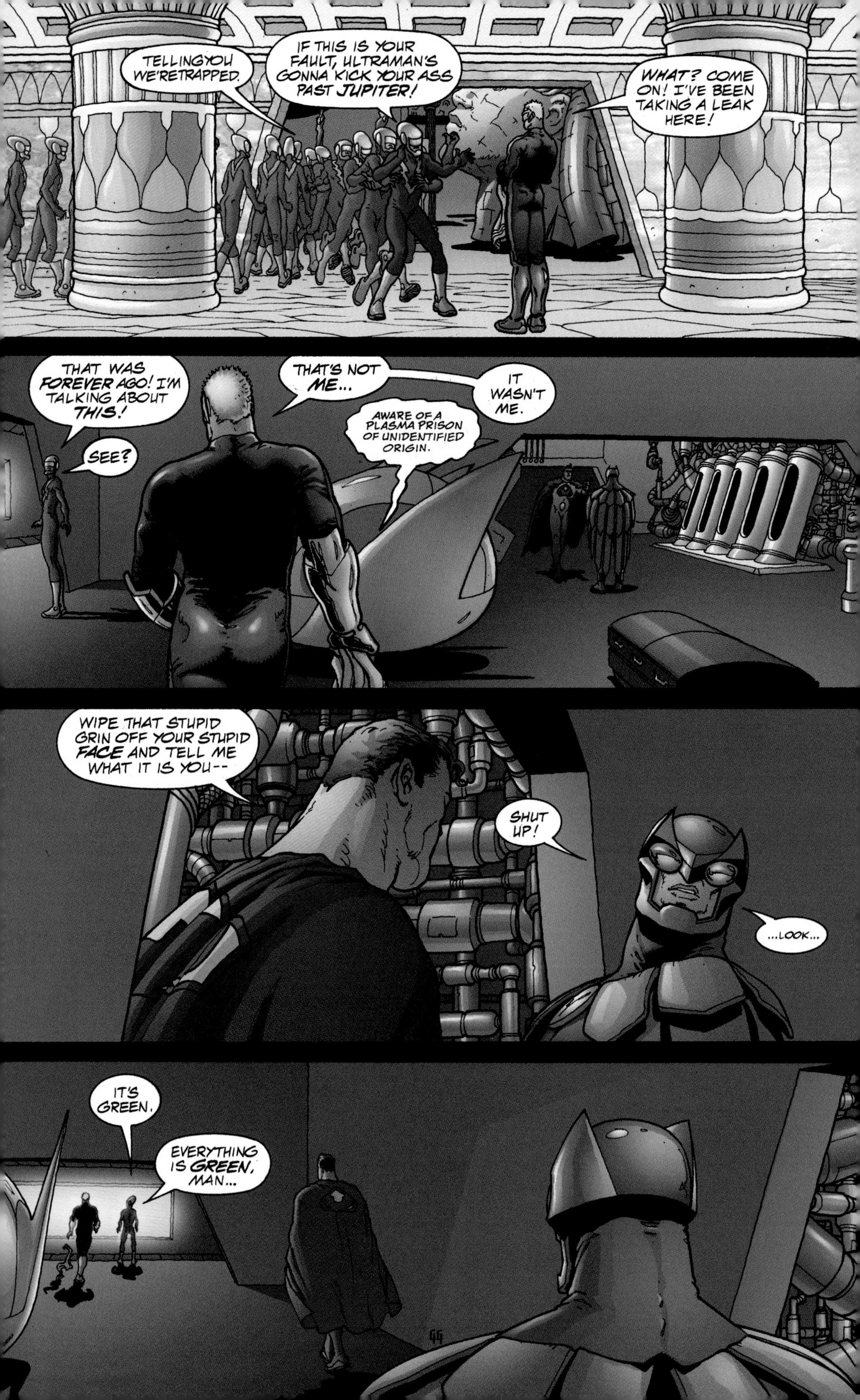
TELLING YOU WE'RE TRAPPED.
IF THIS IS YOUR FAULT, ULTRAMAN'S GONNA KICK YOUR ASS PAST JUPITER!
WHAT? COME ON! I'VE BEEN TAKING A LEAK HERE!
THAT WAS FOREVER AGO! I'M TALKING ABOUT THIS!
SEE?
THAT'S NOT ME...
IT WASN'T ME.
AWARE OF A PLASMA PRISON OF UNIDENTIFIED ORIGIN.
WIPE THAT STUPID GRIN OFF YOUR STUPID FACE AND TELL ME WHAT IT IS YOU--
SHUT UP!
...LOOK...
IT'S GREEN.
EVERYTHING IS GREEN, MAN...
44

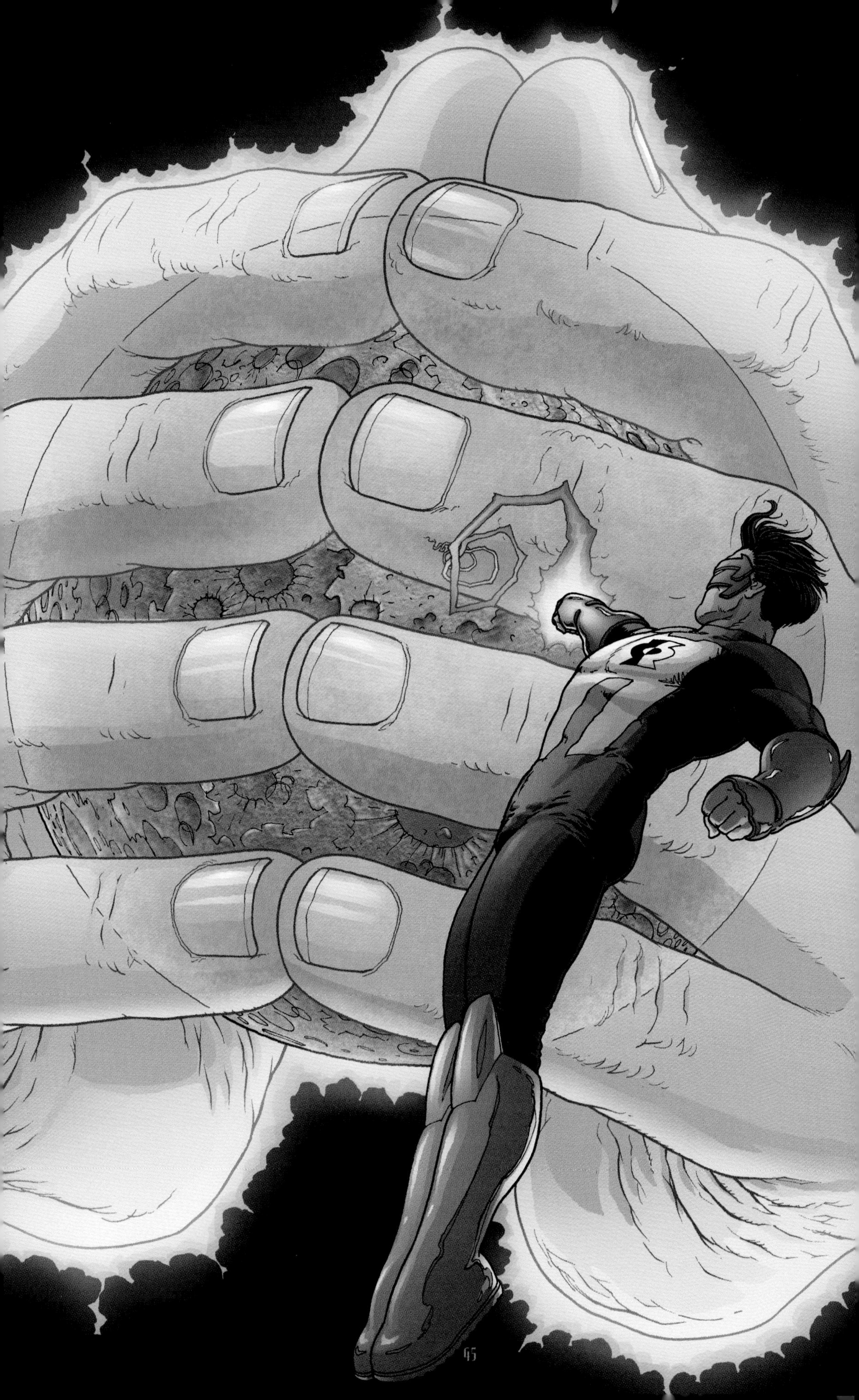

THE MOON'S *WHAT*? GET PICTURES AND *PROVE* IT, FAKE 'EM IF YOU HAVE TO...

I DON'T *CARE* IF IT'S NOT TRUE... I DON'T *CARE* IF IT'LL RUIN YOU.

RECEPTION

DAILY ⊘ PLANET
FREAKSHOW PLANECRASH
HEARTS ON LEFT?

BINGO BIG $$$ BINGO BIG $$$ B

DAILY ⊘ PLANET
FREAKSHOW PLANECRASH
HEARTS ON LEFT?

RECEPTION

DAILY ⊘ PLANET
EUROSTATES TO BOMB EVIL BRITAIN
NUKES FOR NOOKY

DAILY ⊘ PLANET
RIPPER PICS
8 PAGE 3-D INSERT

DAILY ⊘
SEX
SE

DAILY ⊘ PLANET
ELVIS EXECUTION
PAY-FOR-VIEW RECORD

YOU'RE TOMORROW'S *FRONT PAGE*, SWEETHEART.

?

...UH...HI, CAT... I, UH...

I WONDERED IF *LOIS* WAS...

LIEUTENANT CLARK *KENT*? WHAT'S WITH THE *WIMP* ACT, SPACE RANGER?

MARRIAGE TO QUEEN BITCH TURNED YOU GAY?

CAN'T SAY I BLAME YOU.

ANY TIME YOU WANT TO ORBIT SOMETHING A LITTLE LESS *ARCTIC*, JUST WHISTLE.

I SURE WILL. LOIS IS?...

LOIS LANE
EDITOR

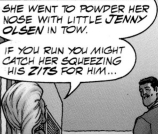

SHE WENT TO POWDER HER NOSE WITH LITTLE *JENNY OLSEN* IN TOW.

IF YOU RUN YOU MIGHT CATCH HER SQUEEZING HIS *ZITS* FOR HIM...

UH... THANKS, CAT. I THINK I KNOW THE WAY.

FREAK.

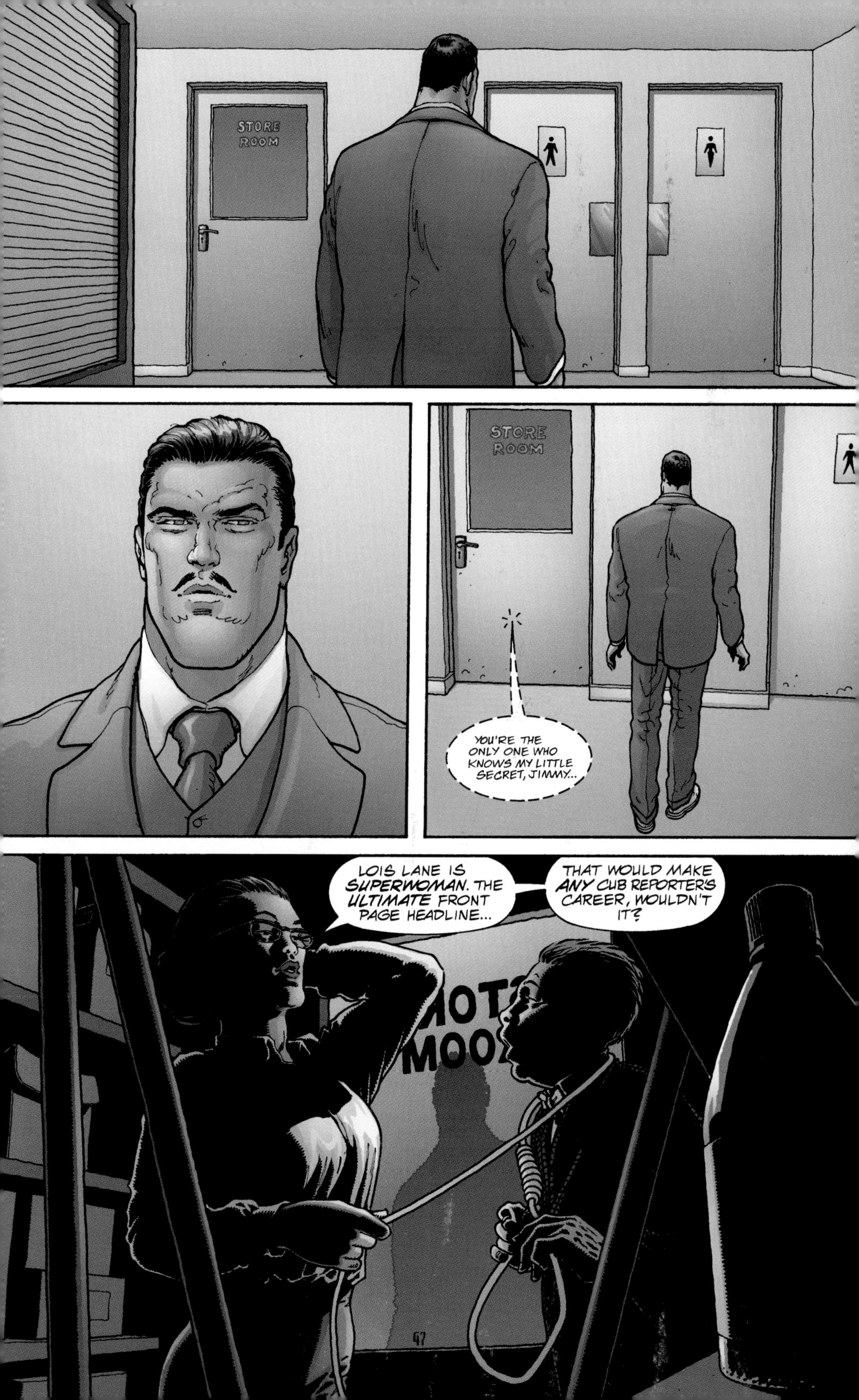
STORE ROOM
STORE ROOM
YOU'RE THE ONLY ONE WHO KNOWS MY LITTLE SECRET, JIMMY...
LOIS LANE IS SUPERWOMAN. THE ULTIMATE FRONT PAGE HEADLINE...
THAT WOULD MAKE ANY CUB REPORTER'S CAREER, WOULDN'T IT?

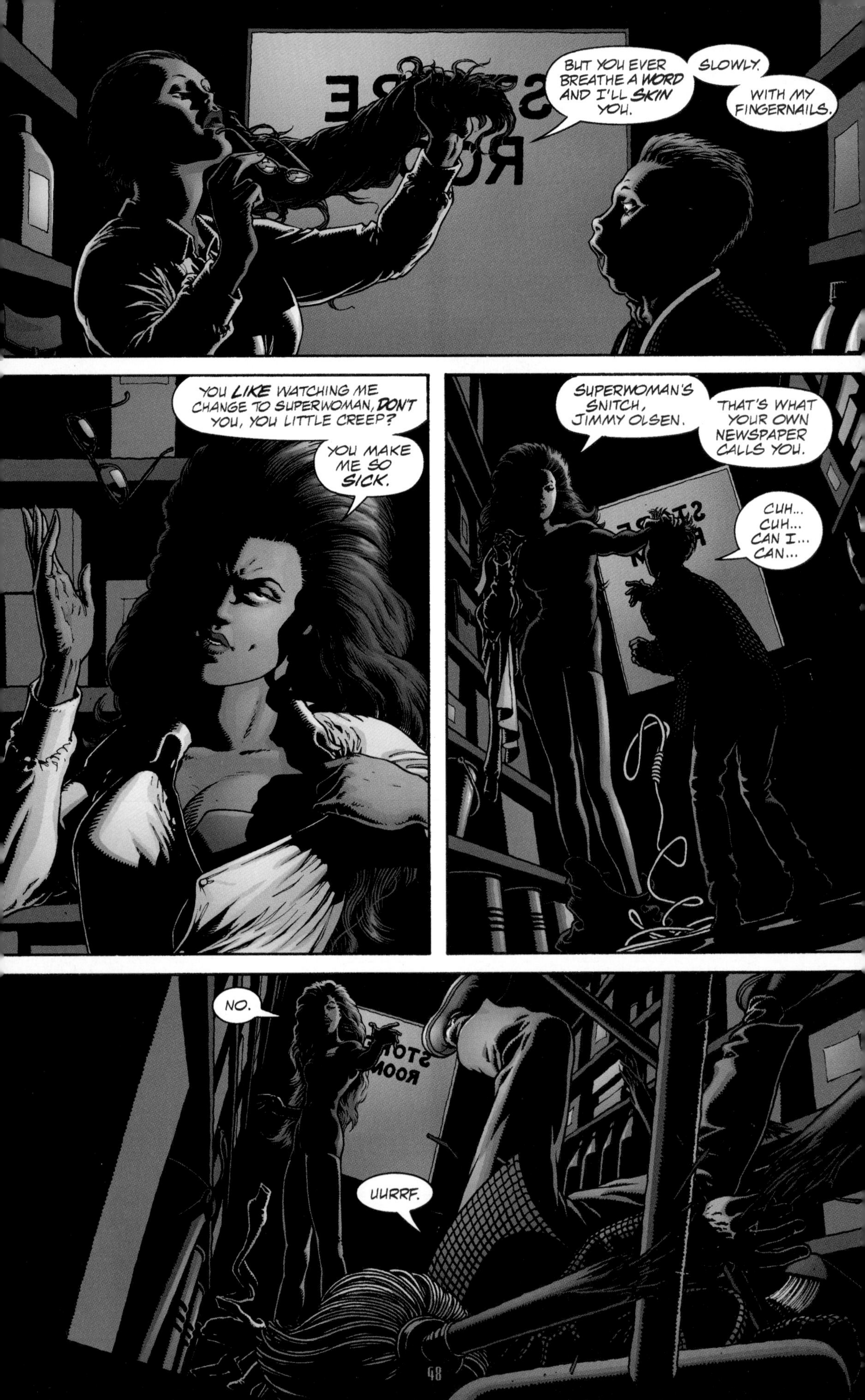
BUT YOU EVER BREATHE A WORD AND I'LL SKIN YOU.
SLOWLY.
WITH MY FINGERNAILS.
YOU LIKE WATCHING ME CHANGE TO SUPERWOMAN, DON'T YOU, YOU LITTLE CREEP?
YOU MAKE ME SO SICK.
SUPERWOMAN'S SNITCH, JIMMY OLSEN.
THAT'S WHAT YOUR OWN NEWSPAPER CALLS YOU.
CUH... CUH... CAN I... CAN...
NO.
UURRF.

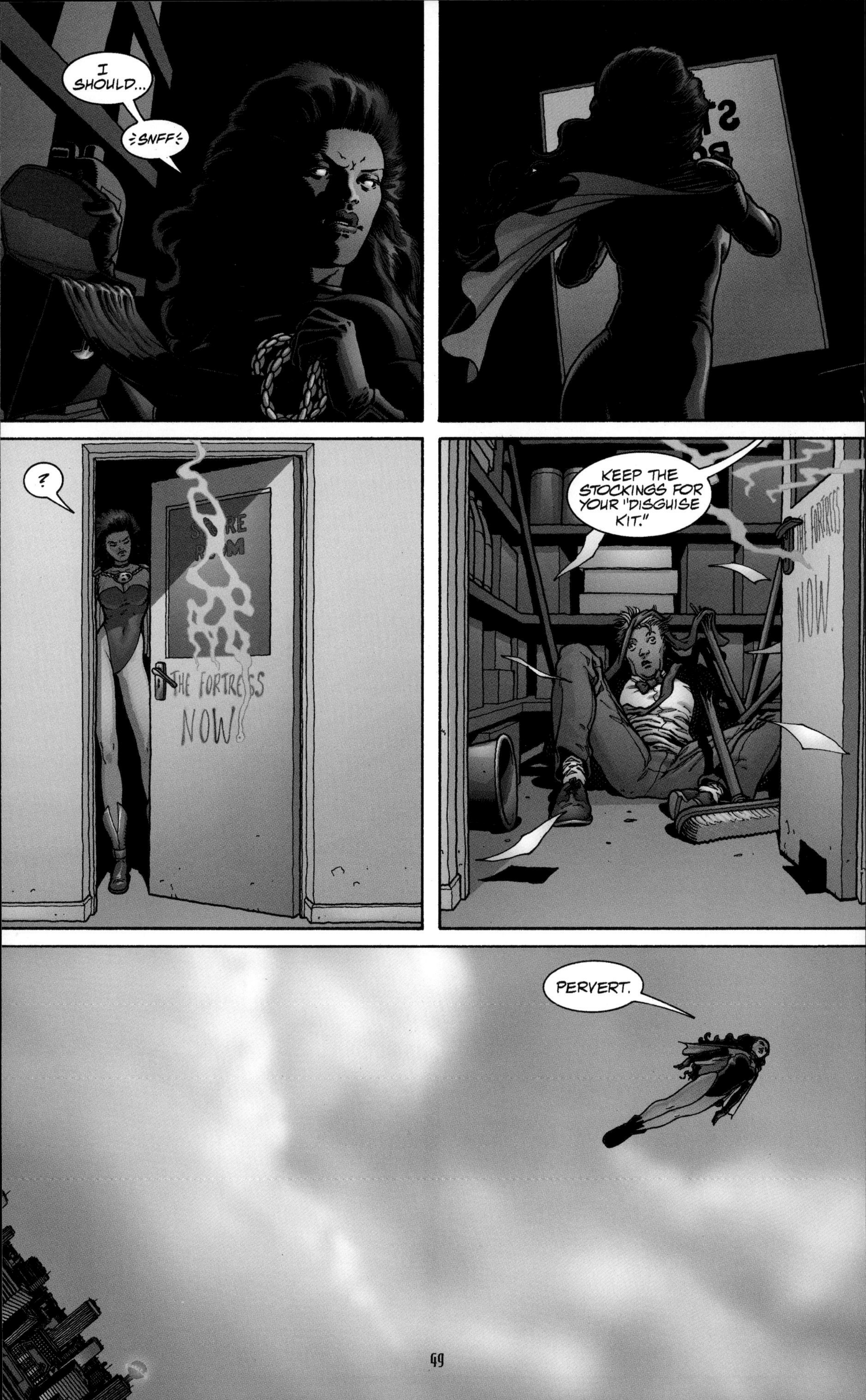
I SHOULD...
SNFF
?
STORE ROOM
THE FORTRESS NOW!
KEEP THE STOCKINGS FOR YOUR "DISGUISE KIT."
THE FORTRESS NOW!
PERVERT.

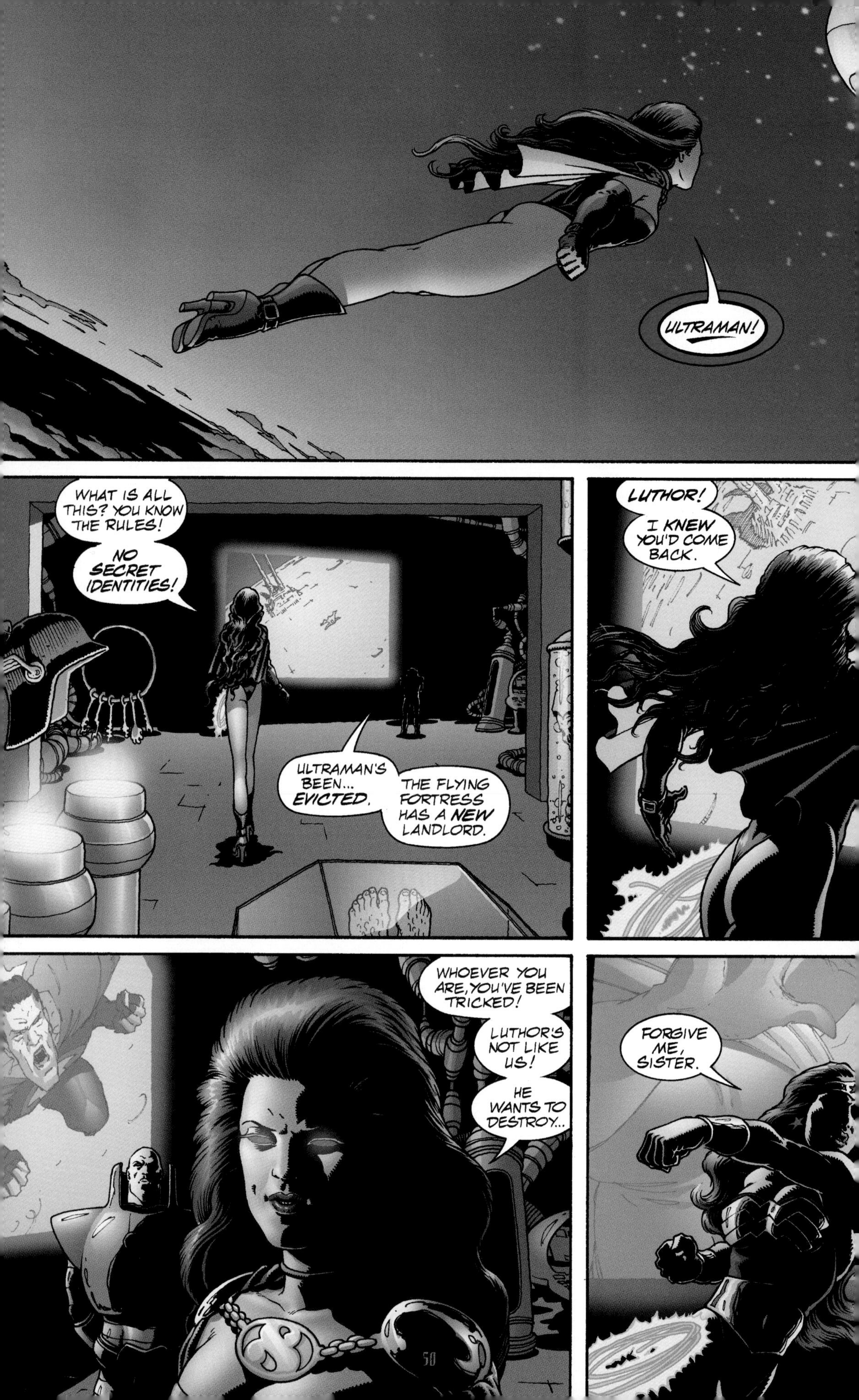
ULTRAMAN!
WHAT IS ALL THIS? YOU KNOW THE RULES!
NO SECRET IDENTITIES!
ULTRAMAN'S BEEN... EVICTED.
THE FLYING FORTRESS HAS A NEW LANDLORD.
LUTHOR!
I KNEW YOU'D COME BACK.
WHOEVER YOU ARE, YOU'VE BEEN TRICKED!
LUTHOR'S NOT LIKE US!
HE WANTS TO DESTROY...
FORGIVE ME, SISTER.

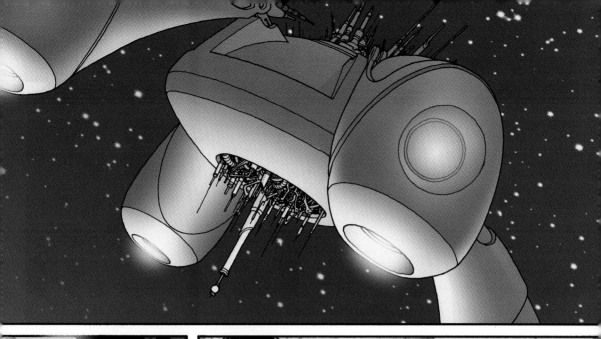

ONCE AGAIN, YOU'VE BEEN PROVEN RIGHT...

IT'S ONLY FAIR TO WARN YOU THAT I DIDN'T COME ALONE.

WHAT?

WAIT... YOU'VE...

WE DON'T WANT TO HURT YOU, SUPERWOMAN.

BUT WE'RE HERE TO STOP YOU.

TUHH

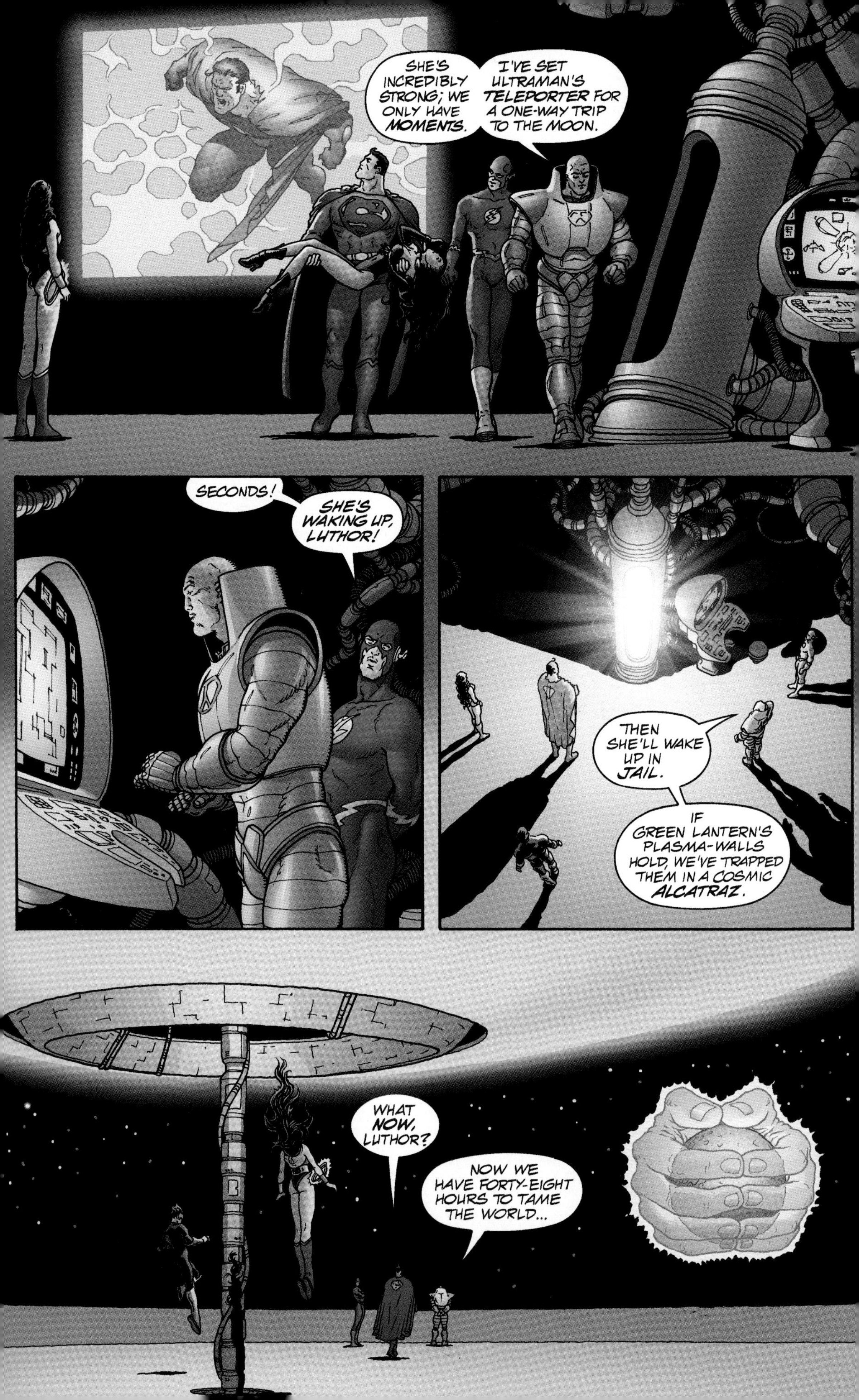
SHE'S INCREDIBLY STRONG; WE ONLY HAVE MOMENTS.
I'VE SET ULTRAMAN'S TELEPORTER FOR A ONE-WAY TRIP TO THE MOON.
SECONDS!
SHE'S WAKING UP, LUTHOR!
THEN SHE'LL WAKE UP IN JAIL.
IF GREEN LANTERN'S PLASMA-WALLS HOLD, WE'VE TRAPPED THEM IN A COSMIC ALCATRAZ.
WHAT NOW, LUTHOR?
NOW WE HAVE FORTY-EIGHT HOURS TO TAME THE WORLD...

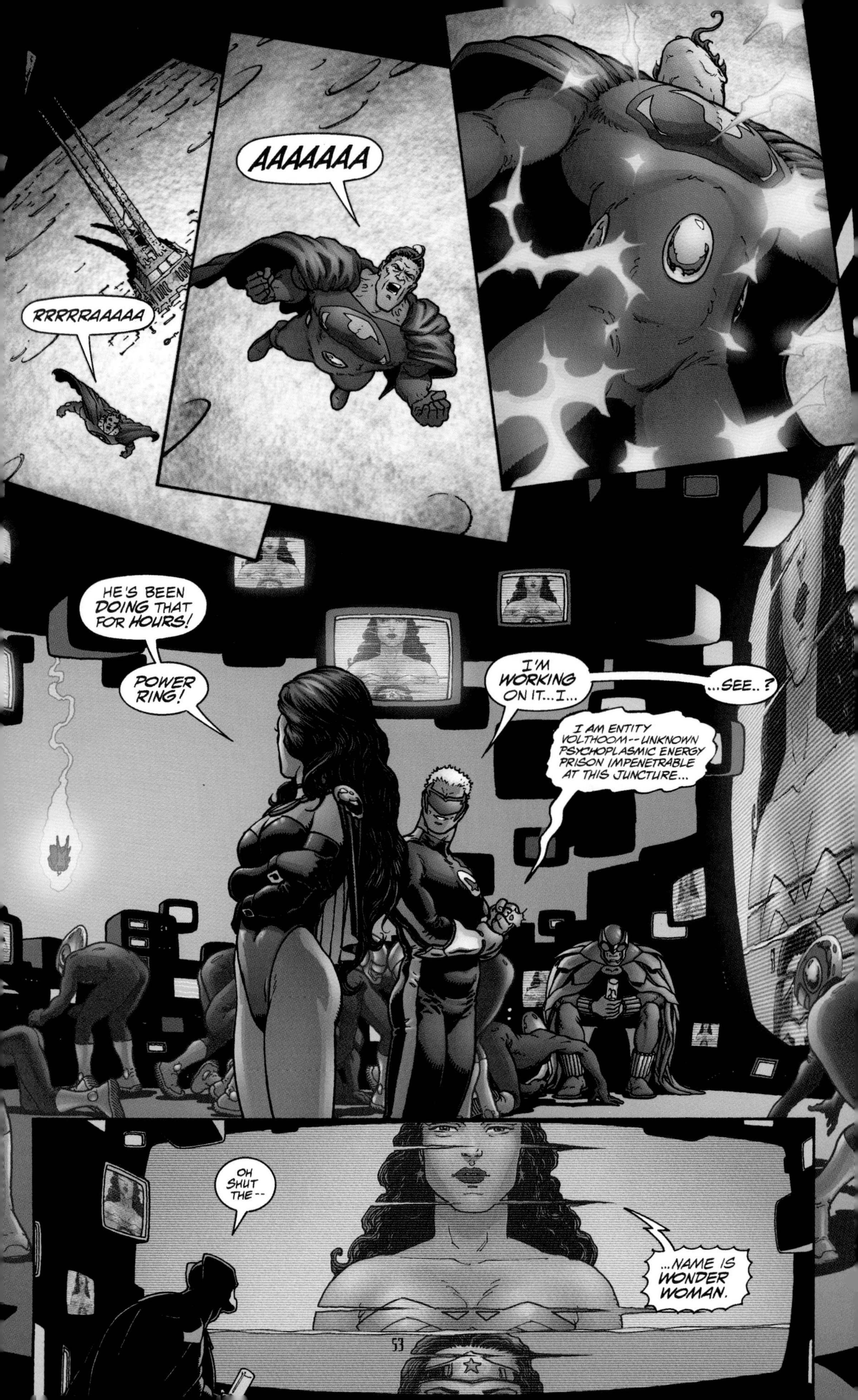
RRRRRAAAAA
AAAAAAA
HE'S BEEN DOING THAT FOR HOURS!
POWER RING!
I'M WORKING ON IT...I...
...SEE..?
I AM ENTITY VOLTHOOM--UNKNOWN PSYCHOPLASMIC ENERGY PRISON IMPENETRABLE AT THIS JUNCTURE...
OH SHUT THE--
...NAME IS WONDER WOMAN.

I REPRESENT THE *JUSTICE LEAGUE OF AMERICA*, FROM A WORLD NOT FAR FROM YOUR OWN BUT VERY DIFFERENT.

WE'RE HERE IN RESPONSE TO A *DISTRESS CALL* FROM ONE OF YOUR PEOPLE, *ALEXANDER LUTHOR.*

WE'VE LEARNED THAT YOURS IS A WORLD CRUSHED BY *TYRANNY,* PARALYZED BY *CRIME* AND CRIPPLED WITH *CORRUPTION* TO THE HIGHEST LEVEL.

WE'VE HEARD THE *CALL* AND *ANSWERED.* THE *SUPER SYNDICATE* IS NO MORE.

LOOK UP AGAIN.

"*JUSTICE*"?

THIS IS A *COUP!*

THE SKIES ARE *SAFE.*

AND WE'RE HERE TO SET YOU *FREE.*

FEEL IT

AMERIKAN VODKA

WHAT'S THE BUZZ?

Tabs IMPERIALS 17 ULTRA NICOTINE

HI TAR   LOW PRICE

CLASS HOPPER

54

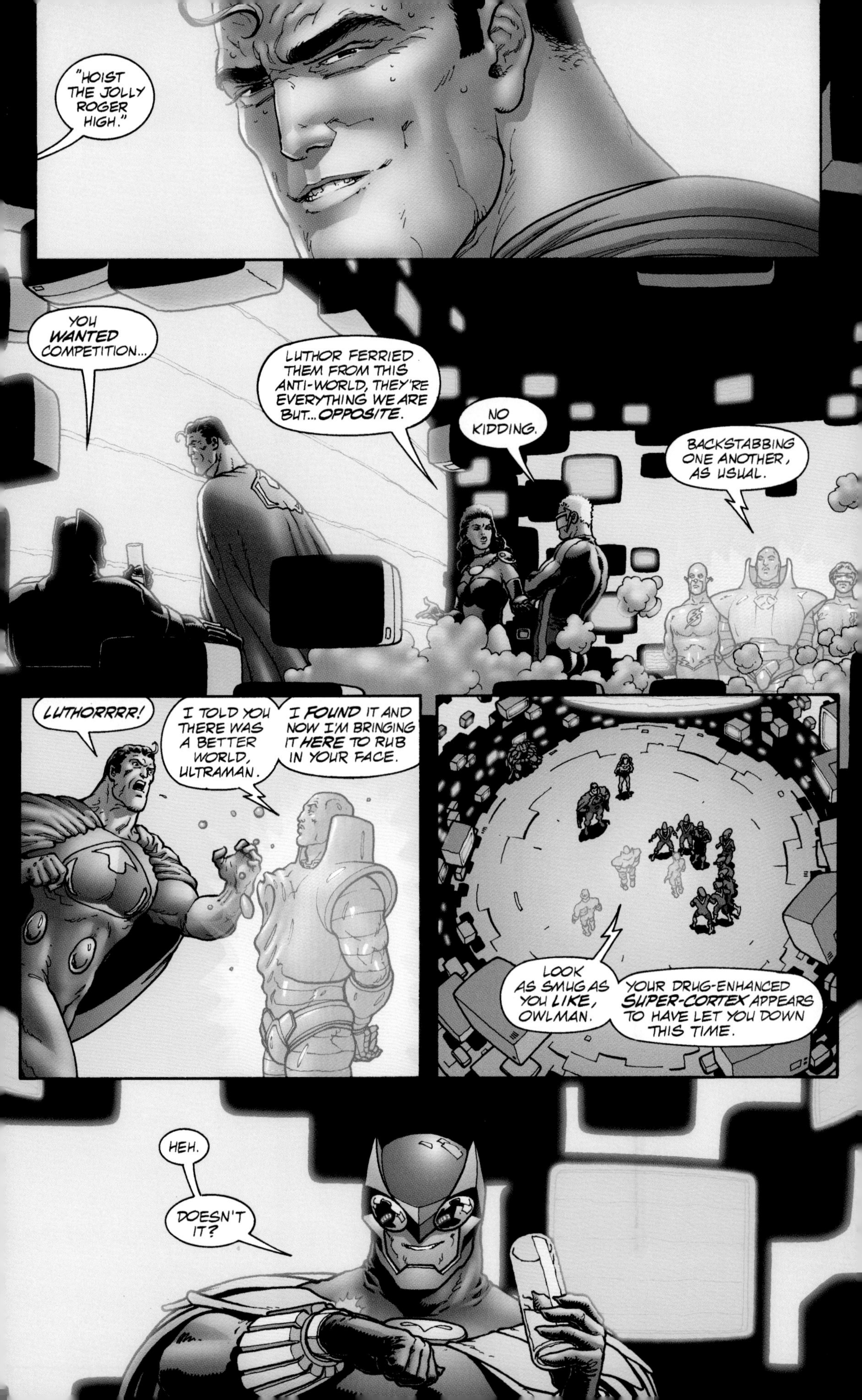
"HOIST THE JOLLY ROGER HIGH."
YOU WANTED COMPETITION...
LUTHOR FERRIED THEM FROM THIS ANTI-WORLD, THEY'RE EVERYTHING WE ARE BUT... OPPOSITE.
NO KIDDING.
BACKSTABBING ONE ANOTHER, AS USUAL.
LUTHORRRR!
I TOLD YOU THERE WAS A BETTER WORLD, ULTRAMAN.
I FOUND IT AND NOW I'M BRINGING IT HERE TO RUB IN YOUR FACE.
LOOK AS SMUG AS YOU LIKE, OWLMAN.
YOUR DRUG-ENHANCED SUPER-CORTEX APPEARS TO HAVE LET YOU DOWN THIS TIME.
HEH.
DOESN'T IT?

WE CAN CONVERT THE **FLYING FORTRESS** INTO A HEADQUARTERS FOR GLOBAL **PEACE**.

BY CAREFULLY COORDINATING THE ABILITIES OF THE **JLA** OVER THE NEXT TWO **DAYS**, WE CAN DISMANTLE THE ENTIRE INFRASTRUCTURE OF THE INTERNATIONAL **SYNDICATES**...

...SO YOU'RE THE **NEW** SYNDICATE, RIGHT. **YOU'RE** THE BOSS NOW...

WE'RE NOT **ANY** KIND OF SYNDICATE, MR. PRESIDENT.

WE CAN **WORK** WITH THAT.

BUT I THOUGHT THIS...

I DON'T **ACCEPT** BRIBES.

I'M AFRAID YOU'LL HAVE TO GET USED TO A NEW WAY OF THINKING.

YOU CAN'T **DO** THIS... THIS VIOLATES SYNDICATE PROTOCOLS...

EVERYTHING HAS CHANGED.

YOUR PROTOCOLS ARE HEREBY **ANNULLED.**

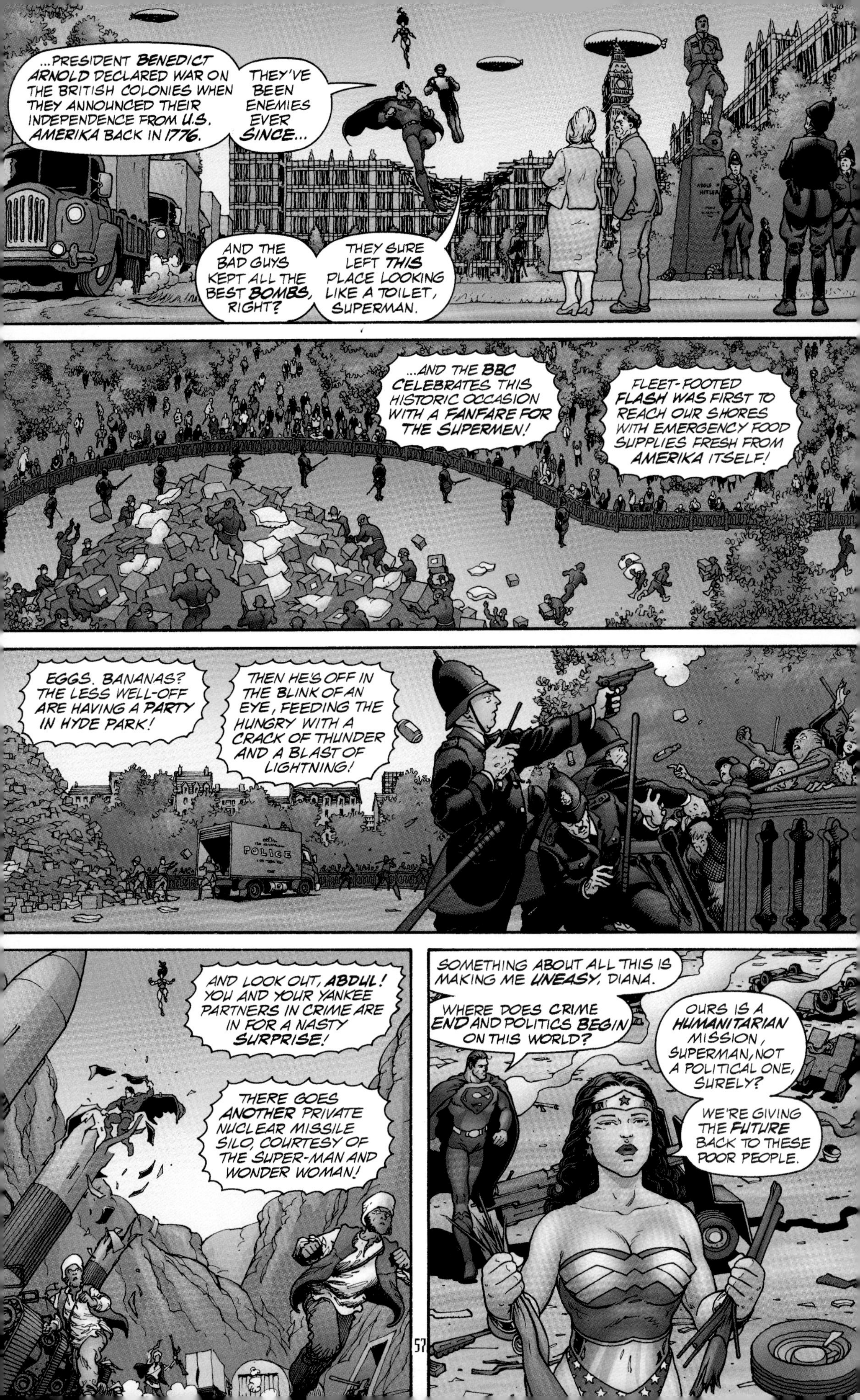
...PRESIDENT BENEDICT ARNOLD DECLARED WAR ON THE BRITISH COLONIES WHEN THEY ANNOUNCED THEIR INDEPENDENCE FROM U.S. AMERIKA BACK IN 1776.
THEY'VE BEEN ENEMIES EVER SINCE...
AND THE BAD GUYS KEPT ALL THE BEST BOMBS, RIGHT?
THEY SURE LEFT THIS PLACE LOOKING LIKE A TOILET, SUPERMAN.
...AND THE BBC CELEBRATES THIS HISTORIC OCCASION WITH A FANFARE FOR THE SUPERMEN!
FLEET-FOOTED FLASH WAS FIRST TO REACH OUR SHORES WITH EMERGENCY FOOD SUPPLIES FRESH FROM AMERIKA ITSELF!
EGGS. BANANAS? THE LESS WELL-OFF ARE HAVING A PARTY IN HYDE PARK!
THEN HE'S OFF IN THE BLINK OF AN EYE, FEEDING THE HUNGRY WITH A CRACK OF THUNDER AND A BLAST OF LIGHTNING!
POLICE
AND LOOK OUT, ABDUL! YOU AND YOUR YANKEE PARTNERS IN CRIME ARE IN FOR A NASTY SURPRISE!
THERE GOES ANOTHER PRIVATE NUCLEAR MISSILE SILO, COURTESY OF THE SUPER-MAN AND WONDER WOMAN!
SOMETHING ABOUT ALL THIS IS MAKING ME UNEASY, DIANA.
WHERE DOES CRIME END AND POLITICS BEGIN ON THIS WORLD?
OURS IS A HUMANITARIAN MISSION, SUPERMAN, NOT A POLITICAL ONE, SURELY?
WE'RE GIVING THE FUTURE BACK TO THESE POOR PEOPLE.

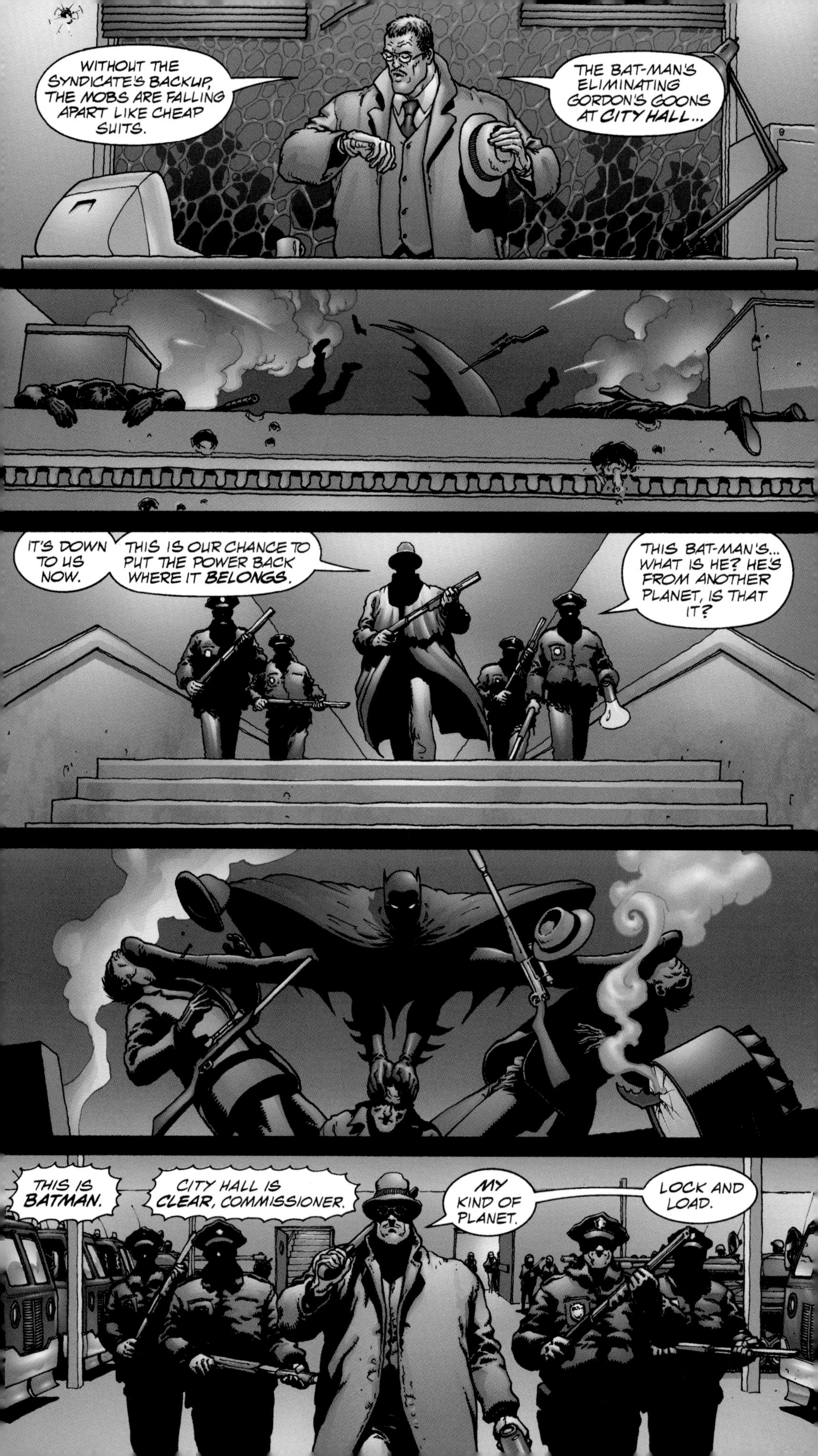
WITHOUT THE SYNDICATE'S BACKUP, THE MOBS ARE FALLING APART LIKE CHEAP SUITS.
THE BAT-MAN'S ELIMINATING GORDON'S GOONS AT CITY HALL...
IT'S DOWN TO US NOW.
THIS IS OUR CHANCE TO PUT THE POWER BACK WHERE IT BELONGS.
THIS BAT-MAN'S... WHAT IS HE? HE'S FROM ANOTHER PLANET, IS THAT IT?
THIS IS BATMAN.
CITY HALL IS CLEAR, COMMISSIONER.
MY KIND OF PLANET.
LOCK AND LOAD.

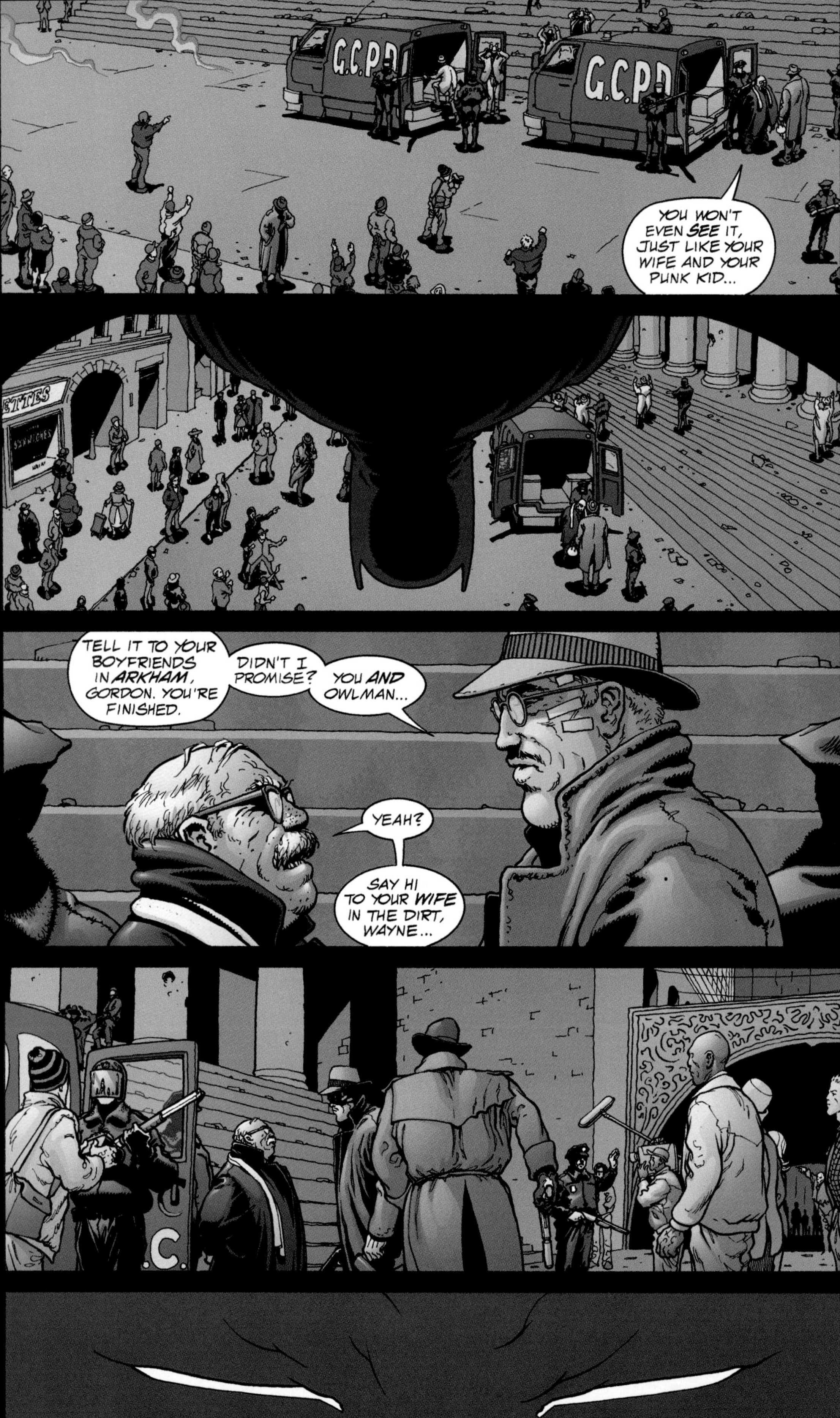
G.C.P.D
G.C.P.D
YOU WON'T EVEN SEE IT, JUST LIKE YOUR WIFE AND YOUR PUNK KID...
ETTES
TELL IT TO YOUR BOYFRIENDS IN ARKHAM, GORDON. YOU'RE FINISHED.
DIDN'T I PROMISE?
YOU AND OWLMAN...
YEAH?
SAY HI TO YOUR WIFE IN THE DIRT, WAYNE...

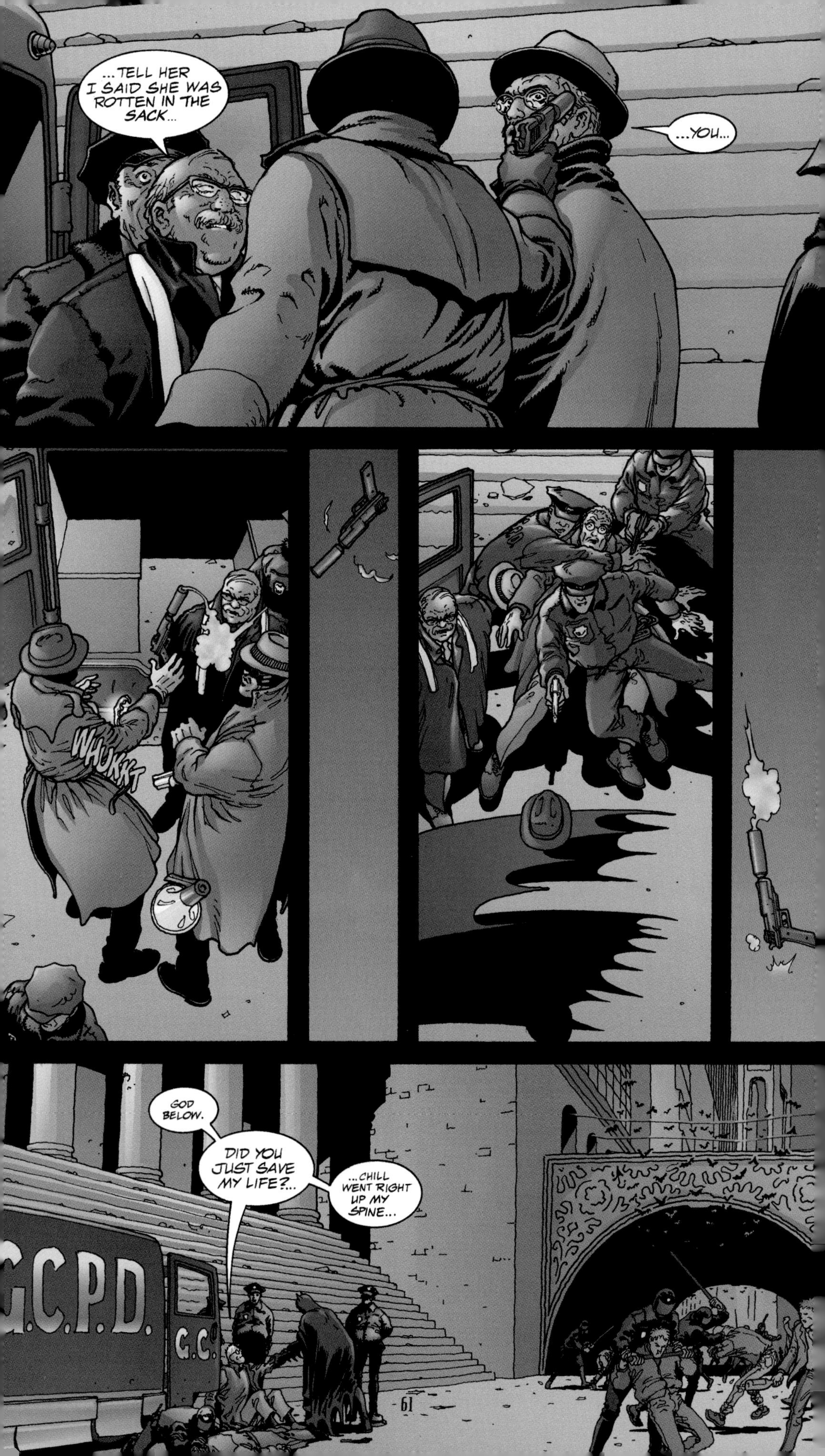
...TELL HER I SAID SHE WAS ROTTEN IN THE SACK...
...YOU...
WHUKKT
GOD BELOW.
DID YOU JUST SAVE MY LIFE?...
...CHILL WENT RIGHT UP MY SPINE...
G.C.P.D.
G.C.

...PEOPLE SHOULD BE MORE *CAREFUL* WITH GUNS.

I FOUND *THIS* ON THE MOON.

MY COLLEAGUES AND I ARE LEAVING HERE SOON. OUR MISSION WAS TO SET AN EXAMPLE...

WHAT ABOUT YOU, COMMISSIONER?

I'M GOING TO BUILD A *NEW* GOTHAM.

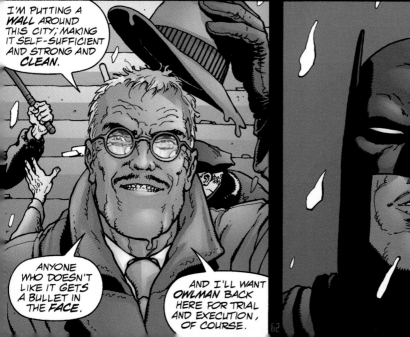

I'M PUTTING A *WALL* AROUND THIS CITY; MAKING IT SELF-SUFFICIENT AND STRONG AND *CLEAN.*

ANYONE WHO DOESN'T LIKE IT GETS A BULLET IN THE *FACE.*

AND I'LL WANT *OWLMAN* BACK HERE FOR TRIAL AND EXECUTION, OF COURSE.

...OF COURSE.

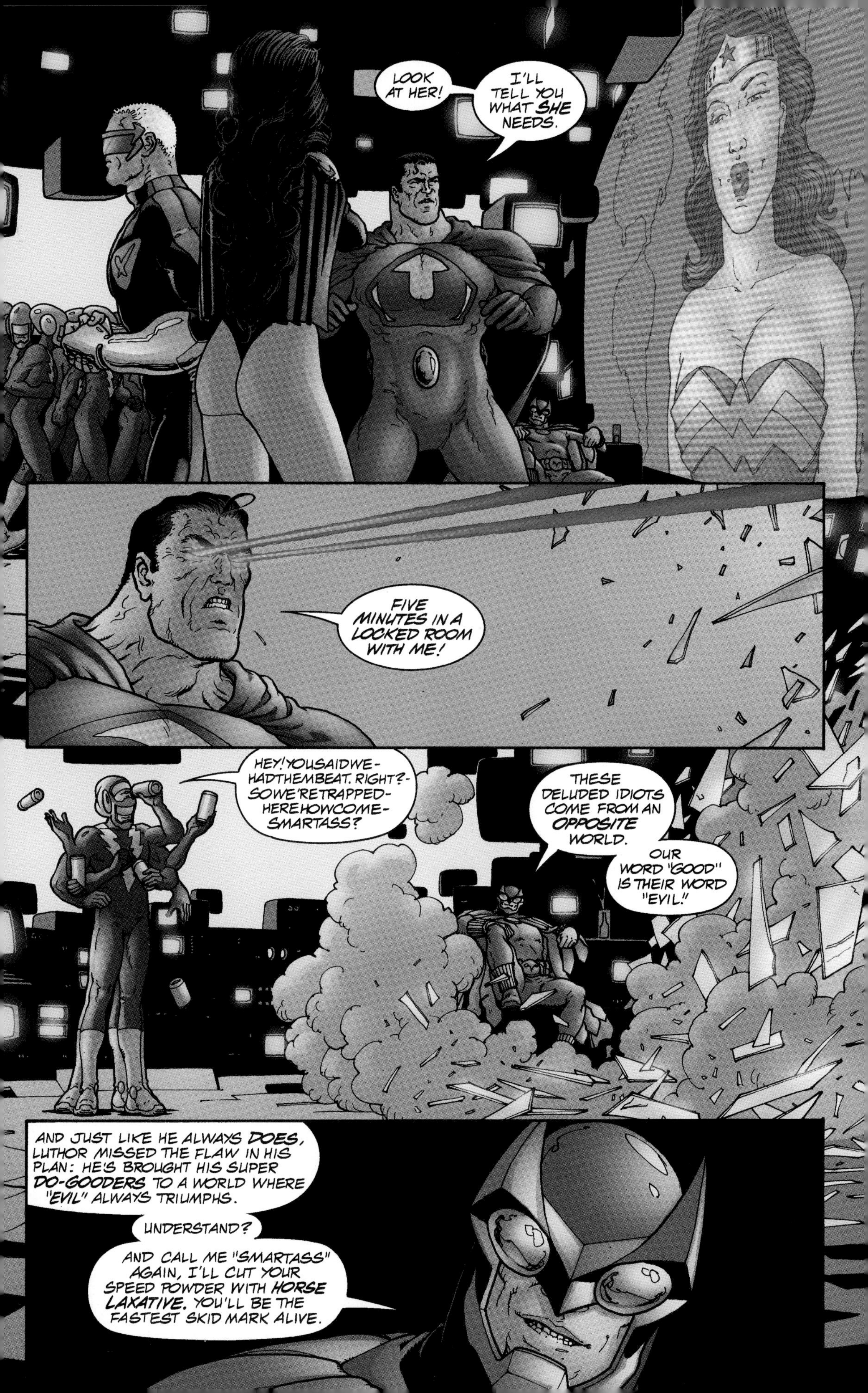
LOOK AT HER!
I'LL TELL YOU WHAT SHE NEEDS.
FIVE MINUTES IN A LOCKED ROOM WITH ME!
HEY! YOUSAIDWE-HADTHEMBEAT. RIGHT?-SOWE'RETRAPPED-HEREHOWCOME-SMARTASS?
THESE DELUDED IDIOTS COME FROM AN OPPOSITE WORLD.
OUR WORD "GOOD" IS THEIR WORD "EVIL."
AND JUST LIKE HE ALWAYS DOES, LUTHOR MISSED THE FLAW IN HIS PLAN: HE'S BROUGHT HIS SUPER DO-GOODERS TO A WORLD WHERE "EVIL" ALWAYS TRIUMPHS.
UNDERSTAND?
AND CALL ME "SMARTASS" AGAIN, I'LL CUT YOUR SPEED POWDER WITH HORSE LAXATIVE. YOU'LL BE THE FASTEST SKID MARK ALIVE.

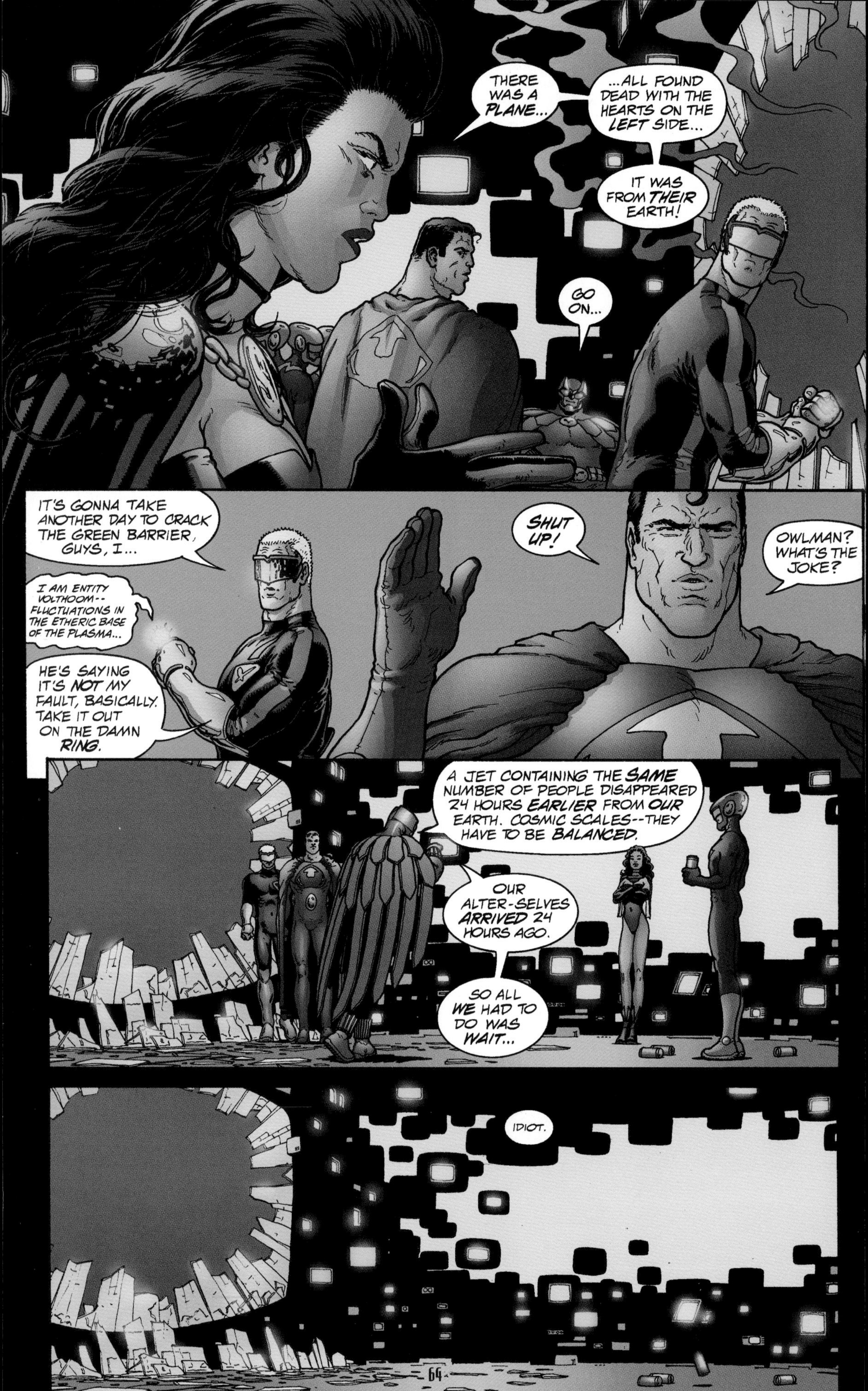
THERE WAS A PLANE...
...ALL FOUND DEAD WITH THE HEARTS ON THE LEFT SIDE...
IT WAS FROM THEIR EARTH!
GO ON...
IT'S GONNA TAKE ANOTHER DAY TO CRACK THE GREEN BARRIER, GUYS, I...
I AM ENTITY VOLTHOOM-- FLUCTUATIONS IN THE ETHERIC BASE OF THE PLASMA...
HE'S SAYING IT'S NOT MY FAULT, BASICALLY. TAKE IT OUT ON THE DAMN RING.
SHUT UP!
OWLMAN? WHAT'S THE JOKE?
A JET CONTAINING THE SAME NUMBER OF PEOPLE DISAPPEARED 24 HOURS EARLIER FROM OUR EARTH. COSMIC SCALES--THEY HAVE TO BE BALANCED.
OUR ALTER-SELVES ARRIVED 24 HOURS AGO.
SO ALL WE HAD TO DO WAS WAIT...
IDIOT.

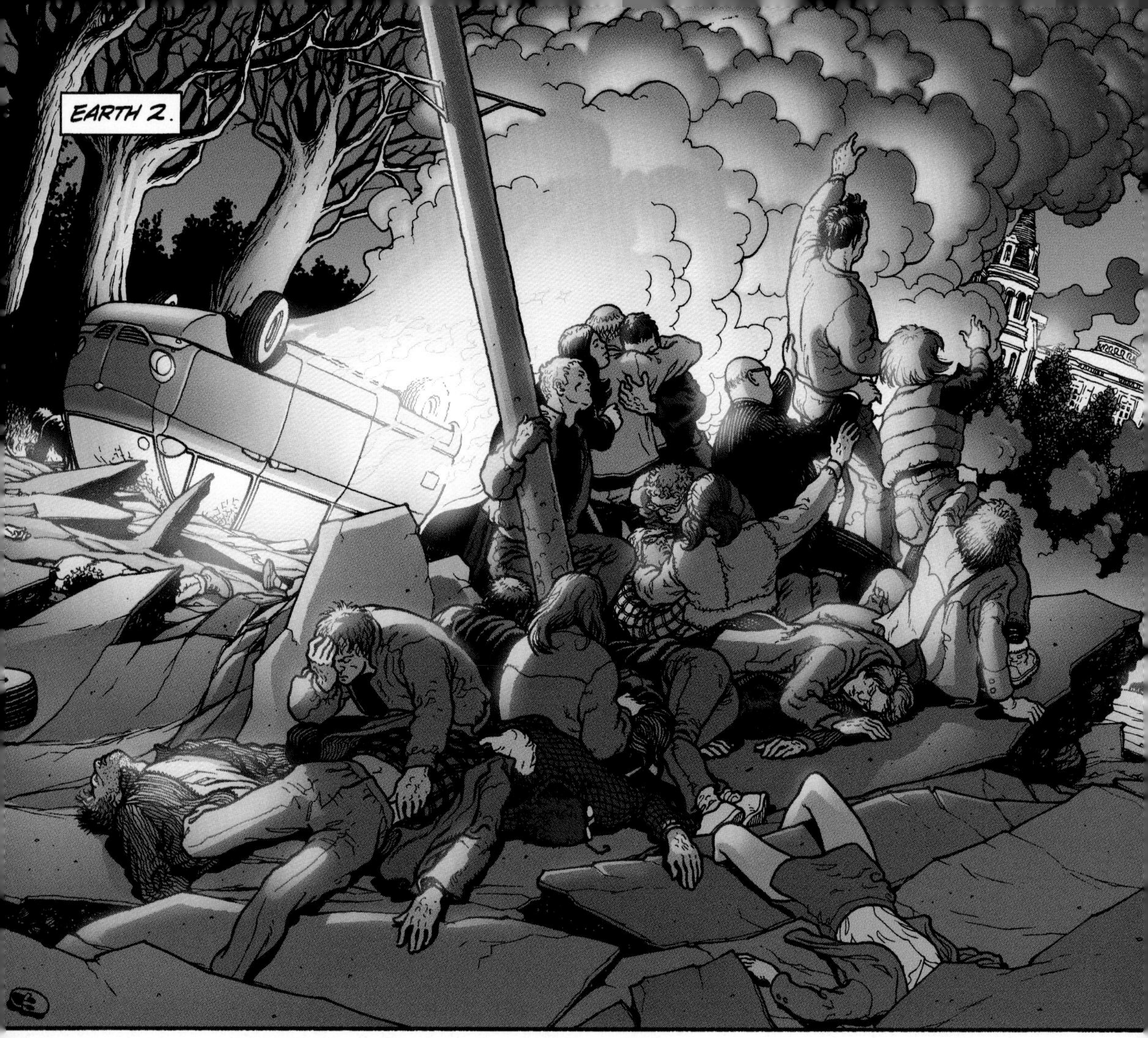
EARTH 2.

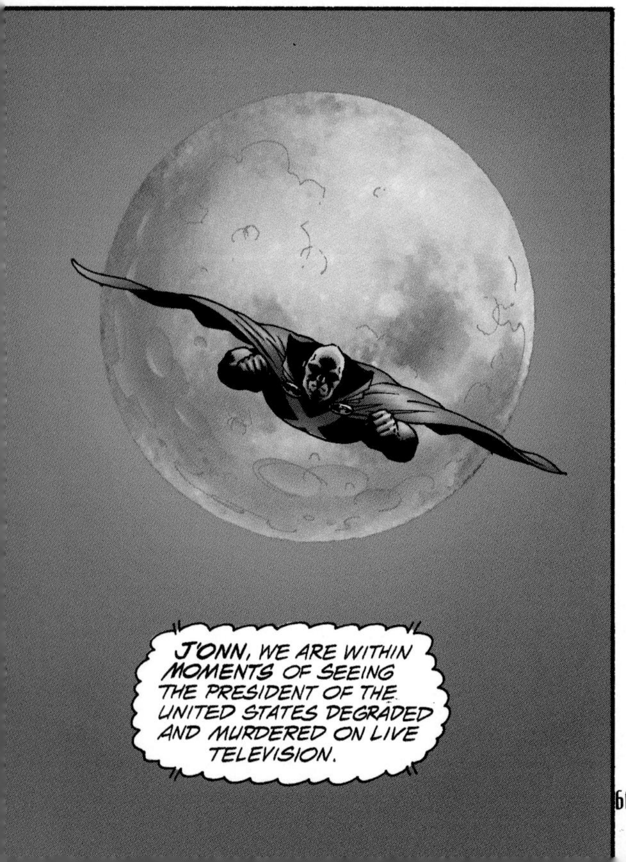
J'ONN, WE ARE WITHIN MOMENTS OF SEEING THE PRESIDENT OF THE UNITED STATES DEGRADED AND MURDERED ON LIVE TELEVISION.

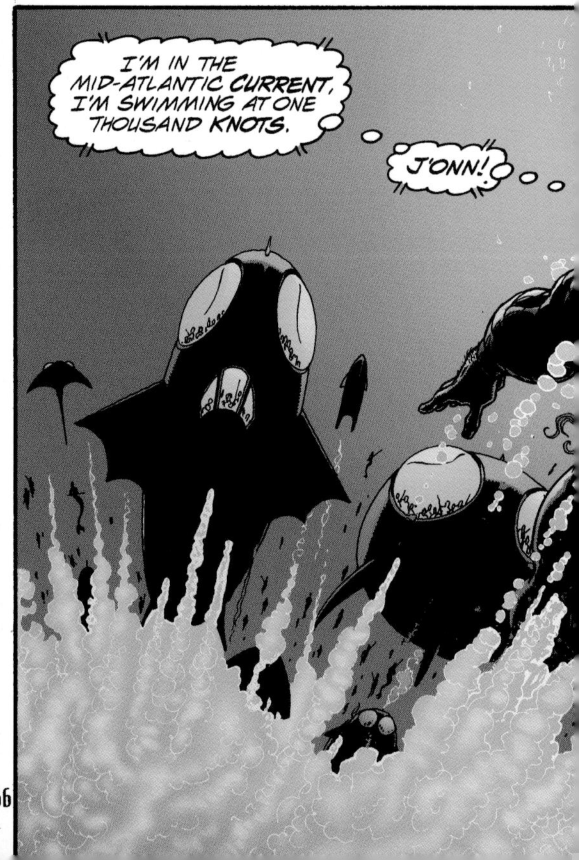
I'M IN THE MID-ATLANTIC CURRENT, I'M SWIMMING AT ONE THOUSAND KNOTS.
J'ONN!

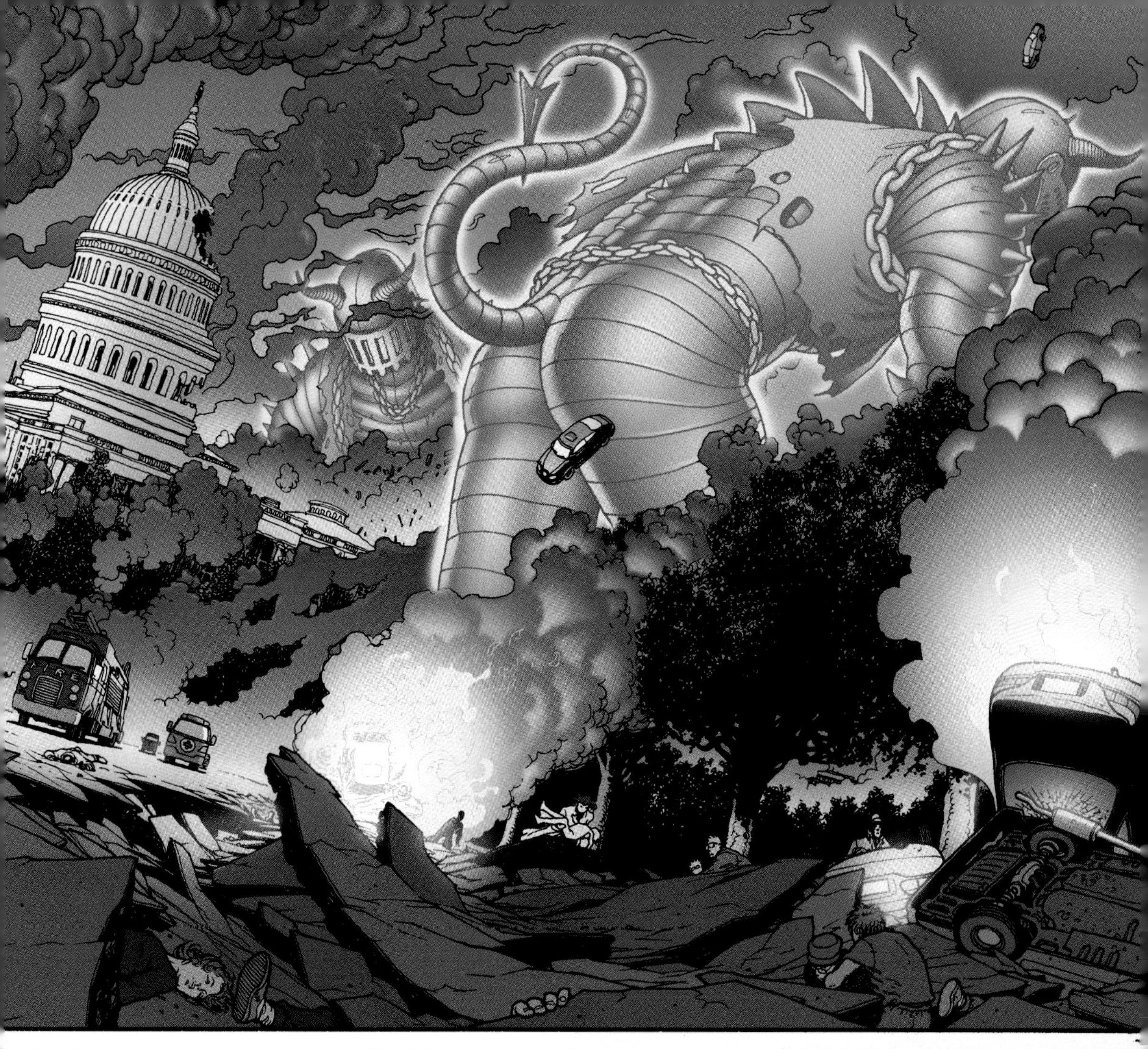

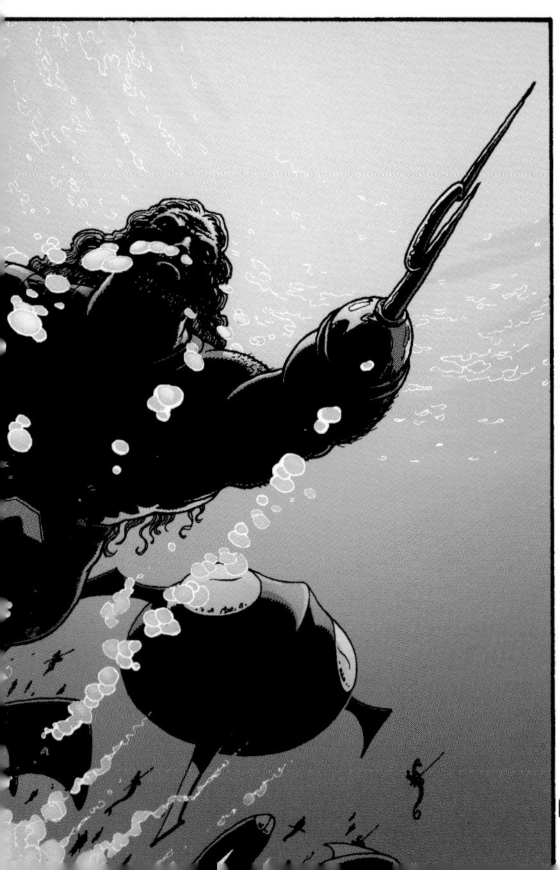

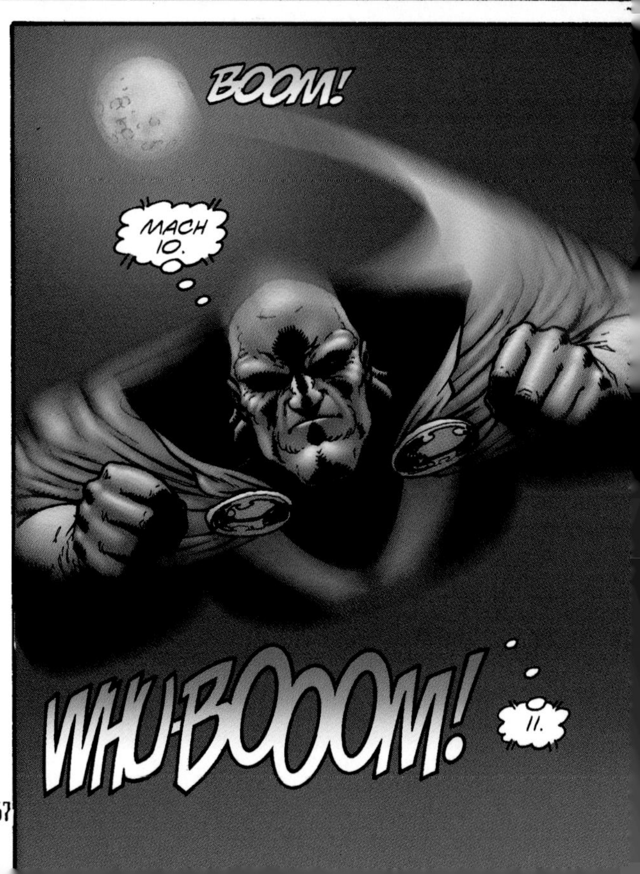
BOOM!
MACH 10.
WHU-BOOOM!
!!.

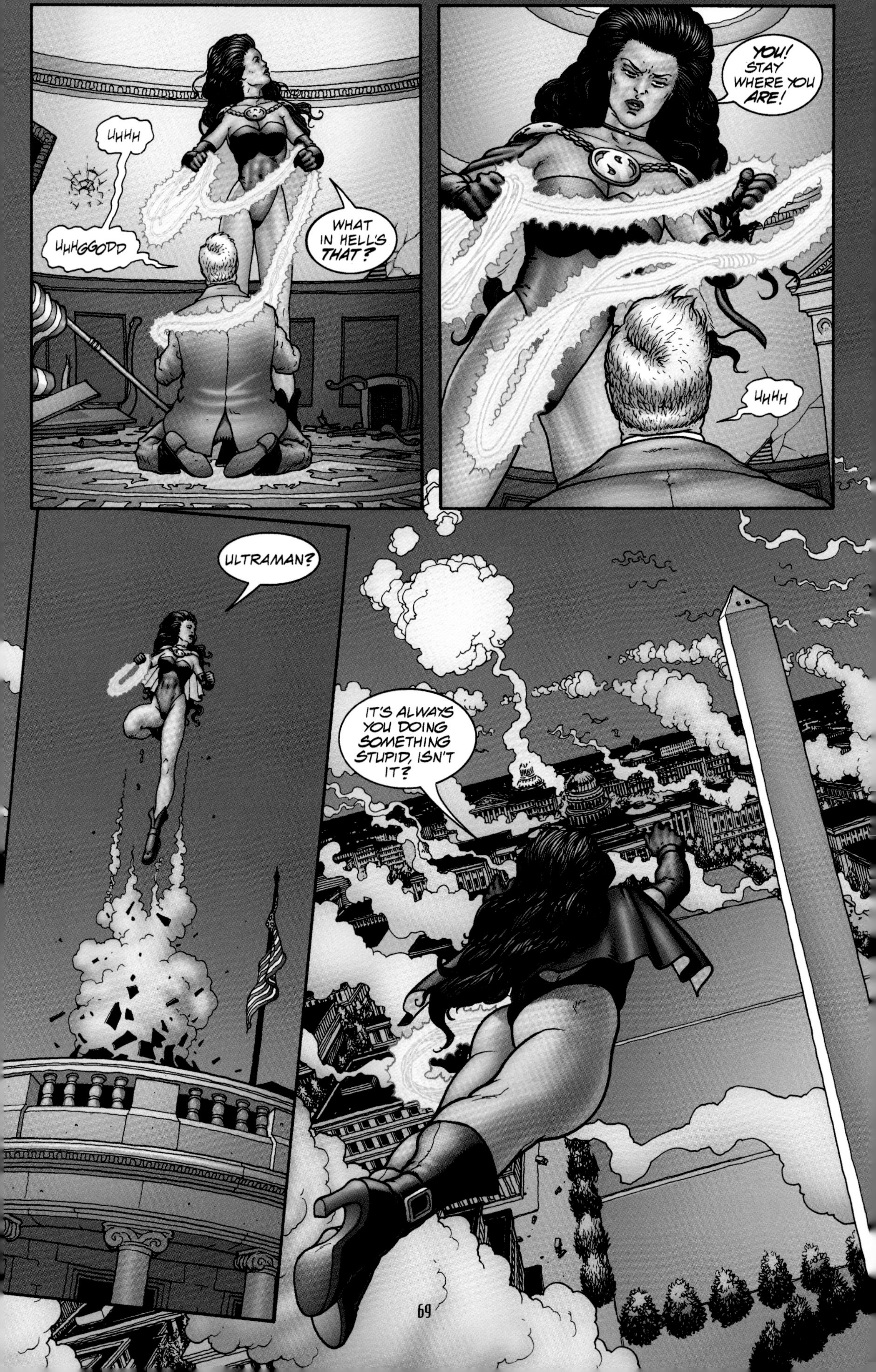
UHHH
UHHGGODD
WHAT IN HELL'S THAT?
YOU! STAY WHERE YOU ARE!
UHHH
ULTRAMAN?
IT'S ALWAYS YOU DOING SOMETHING STUPID, ISN'T IT?

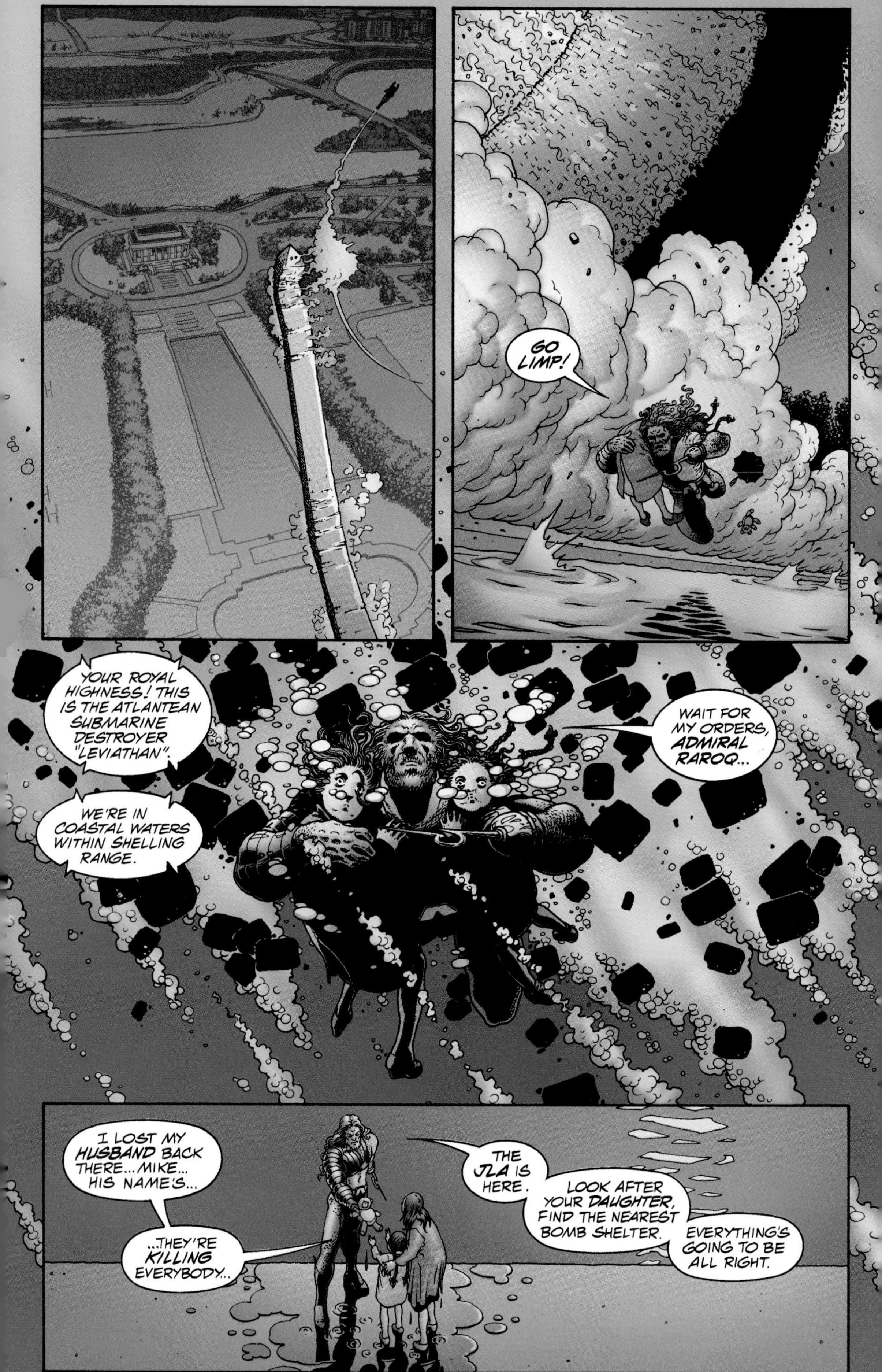
GO LIMP!
YOUR ROYAL HIGHNESS! THIS IS THE ATLANTEAN SUBMARINE DESTROYER "LEVIATHAN".
WE'RE IN COASTAL WATERS WITHIN SHELLING RANGE.
WAIT FOR MY ORDERS, ADMIRAL RAROQ...
I LOST MY HUSBAND BACK THERE...MIKE... HIS NAME'S...
...THEY'RE KILLING EVERYBODY...
THE JLA IS HERE.
LOOK AFTER YOUR DAUGHTER, FIND THE NEAREST BOMB SHELTER.
EVERYTHING'S GOING TO BE ALL RIGHT.

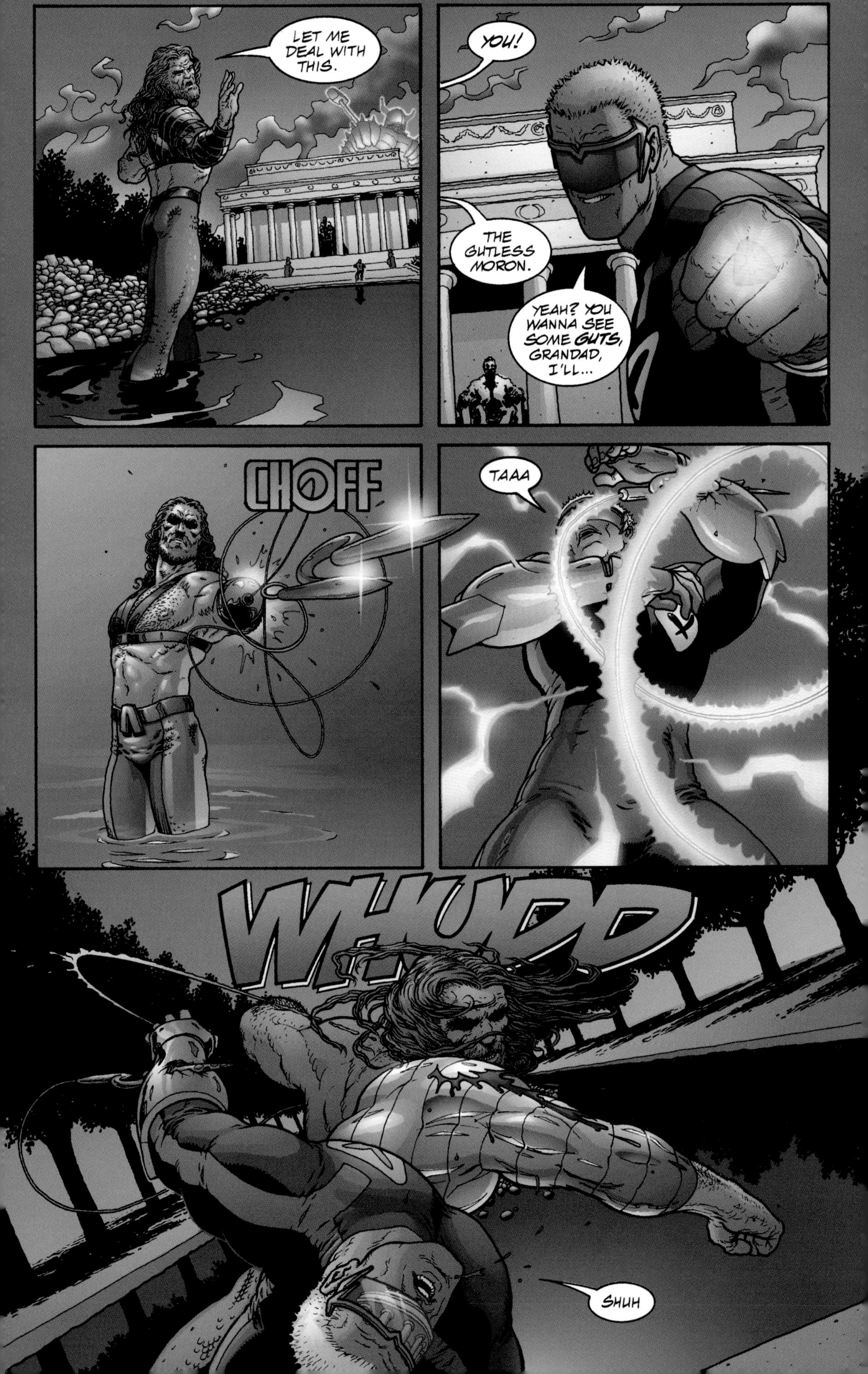
LET ME DEAL WITH THIS.
YOU!
THE GUTLESS MORON.
YEAH? YOU WANNA SEE SOME GUTS, GRANDAD, I'LL...
CHOFF
TAAA
WHUDD
SHUH

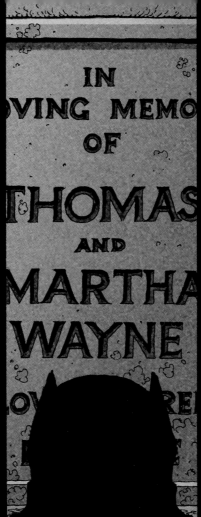

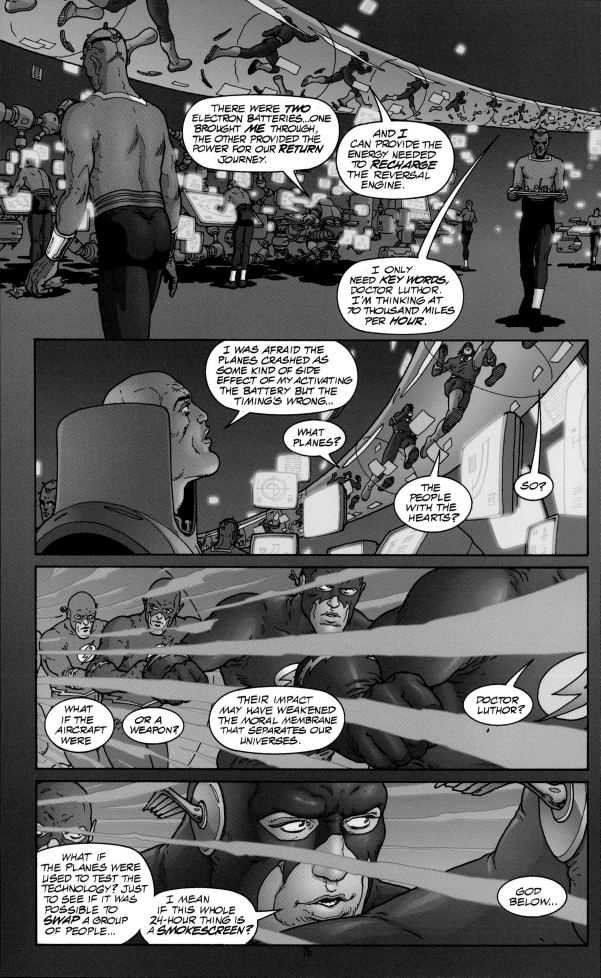

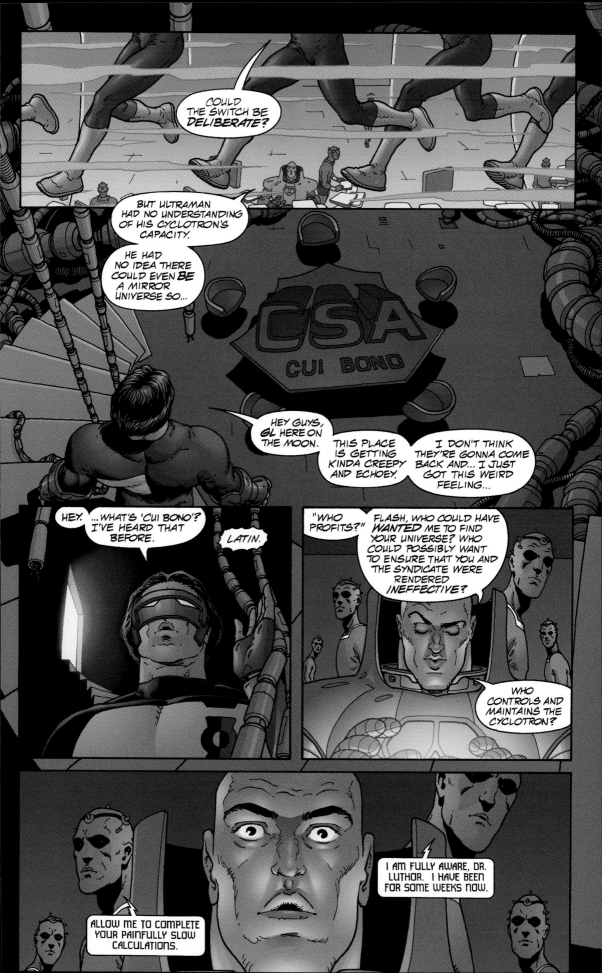

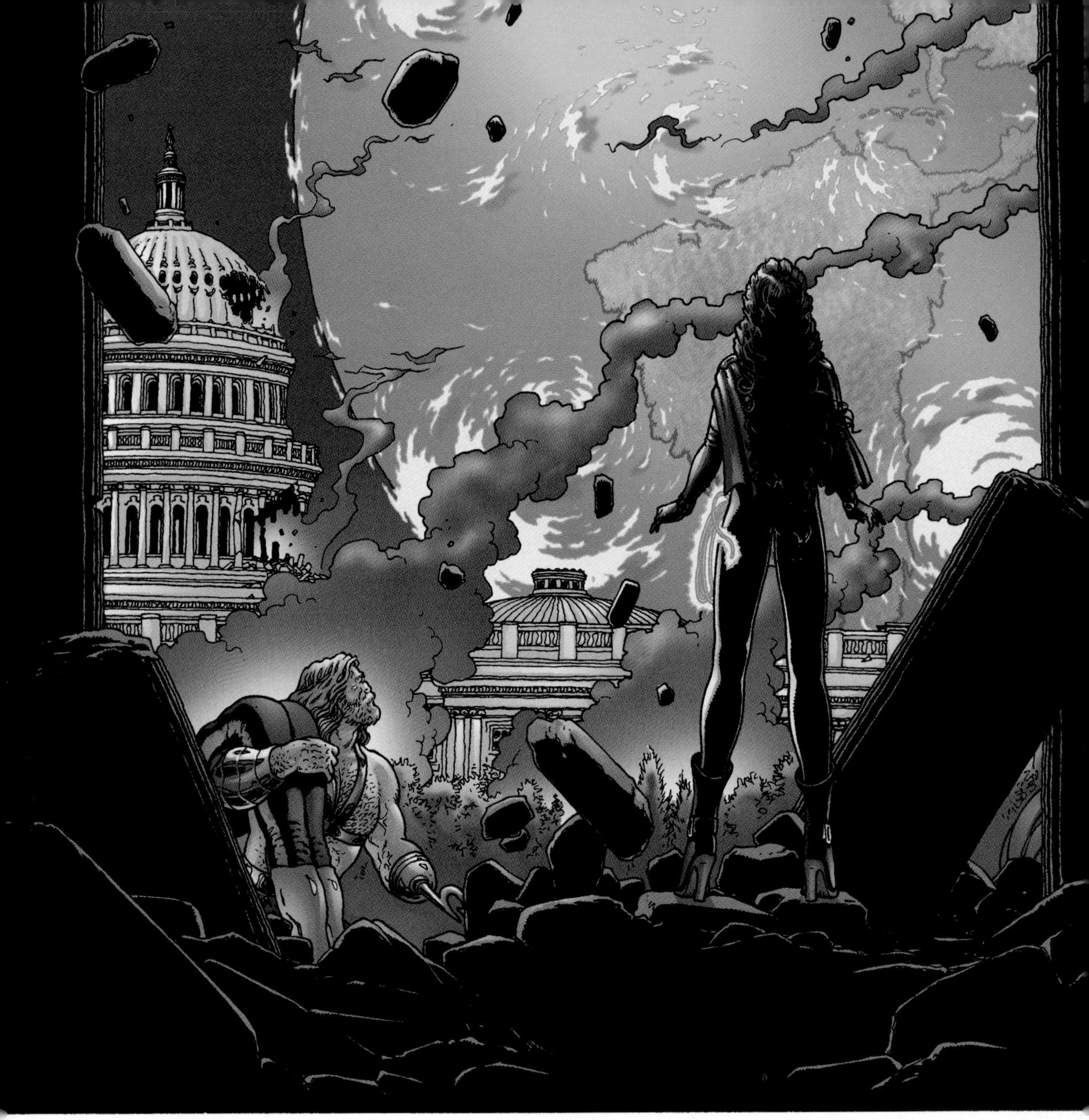

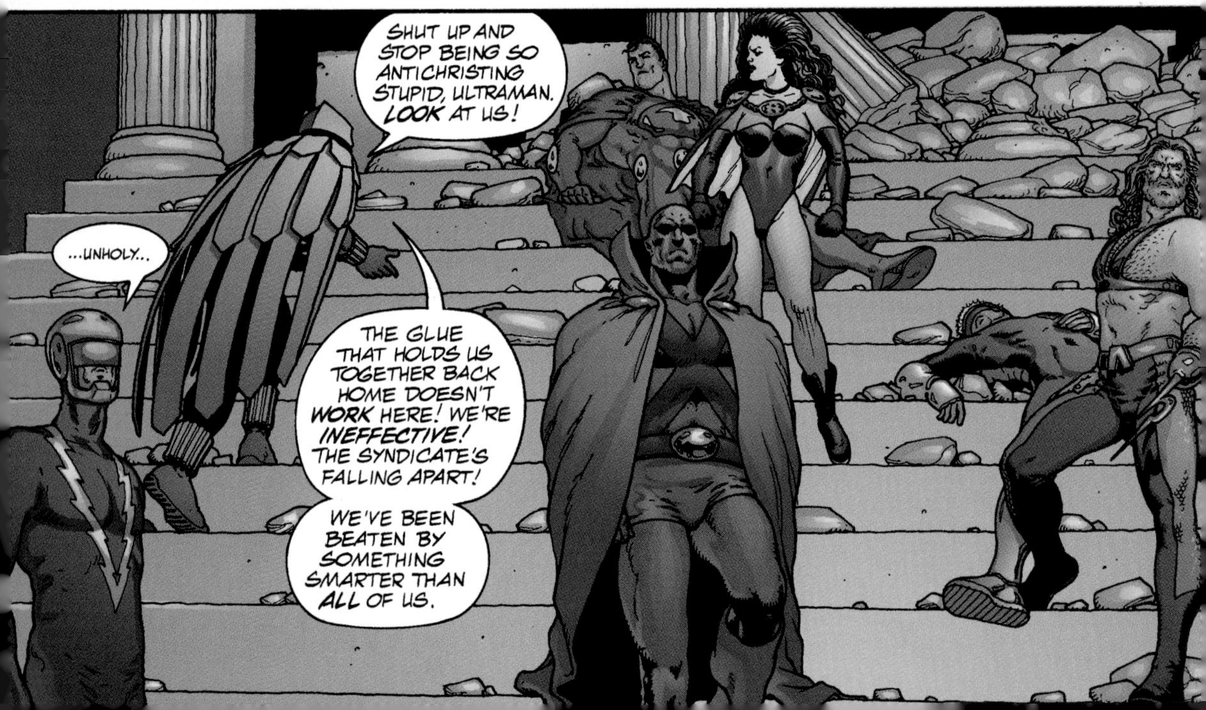
SHUT UP AND STOP BEING SO ANTICHRISTING STUPID, ULTRAMAN. LOOK AT US!
...UNHOLY...
THE GLUE THAT HOLDS US TOGETHER BACK HOME DOESN'T WORK HERE! WE'RE INEFFECTIVE! THE SYNDICATE'S FALLING APART!
WE'VE BEEN BEATEN BY SOMETHING SMARTER THAN ALL OF US.

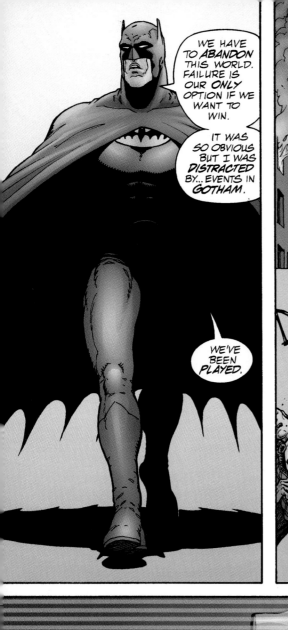

WE HAVE TO **ABANDON** THIS WORLD. FAILURE IS OUR **ONLY** OPTION IF WE WANT TO WIN.

IT WAS SO OBVIOUS BUT I WAS **DISTRACTED** BY... EVENTS IN **GOTHAM**.

WE'VE BEEN **PLAYED**.

I'LL DO WHAT I CAN WITH **BRAINIAC**.

WE **FAILED** THEM. WE FAILED **LUTHOR**.

ONLY BECAUSE OUR METHODS **CAN'T** SUCCEED ON THIS WORLD. IT'S A LAW OF NATURE; EVERYTHING WE DO IS **ORDAINED** TO FAIL.

EVEN **GOOD** DEEDS GO BAD HERE, **DIANA**.

DOWN WITH THE JUSTICE LEAG

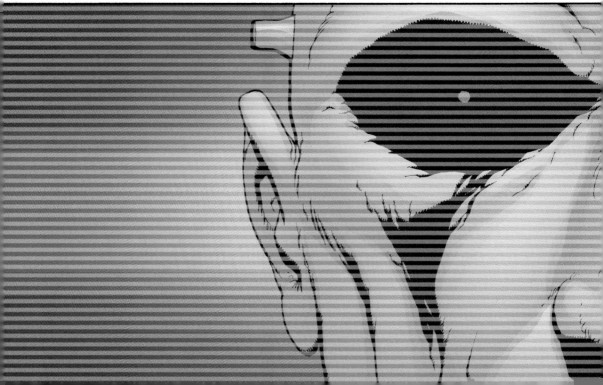

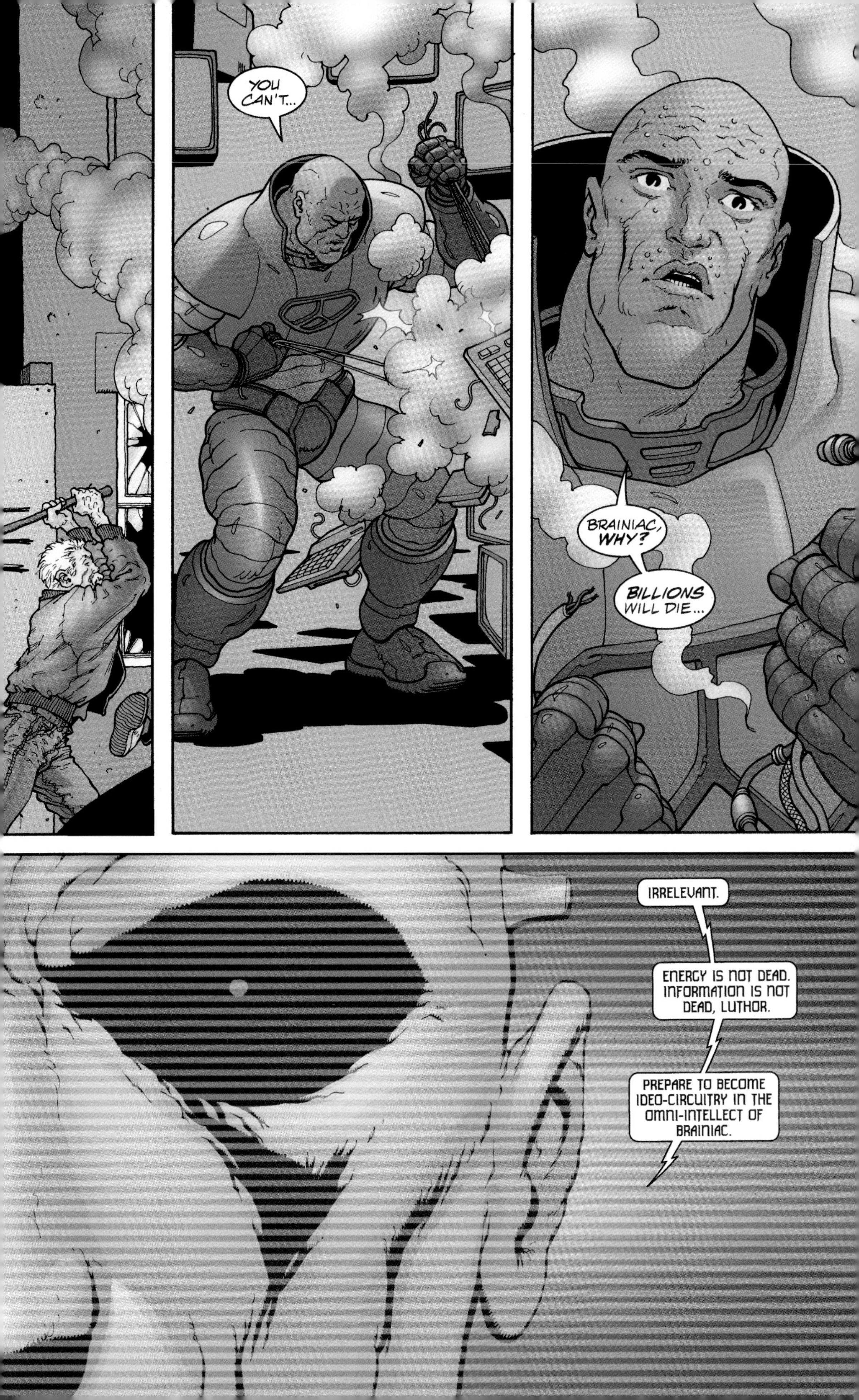

YOU CAN'T...
BRAINIAC, WHY?
BILLIONS WILL DIE...
IRRELEVANT.
ENERGY IS NOT DEAD. INFORMATION IS NOT DEAD, LUTHOR.
PREPARE TO BECOME IDEO-CIRCUITRY IN THE OMNI-INTELLECT OF BRAINIAC.

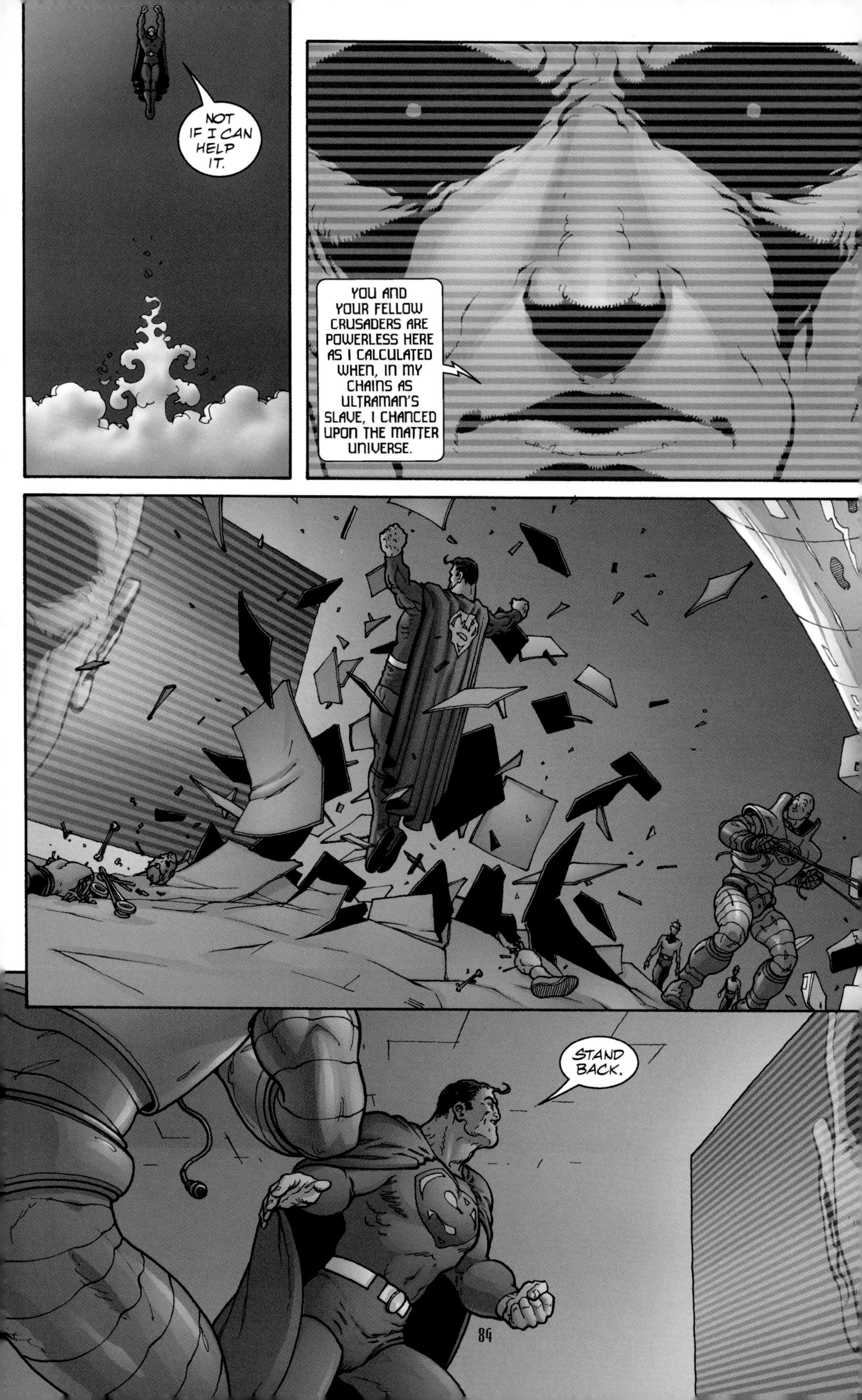

NOT IF I CAN HELP IT.
YOU AND YOUR FELLOW CRUSADERS ARE POWERLESS HERE AS I CALCULATED WHEN, IN MY CHAINS AS ULTRAMAN'S SLAVE, I CHANCED UPON THE MATTER UNIVERSE.
STAND BACK.

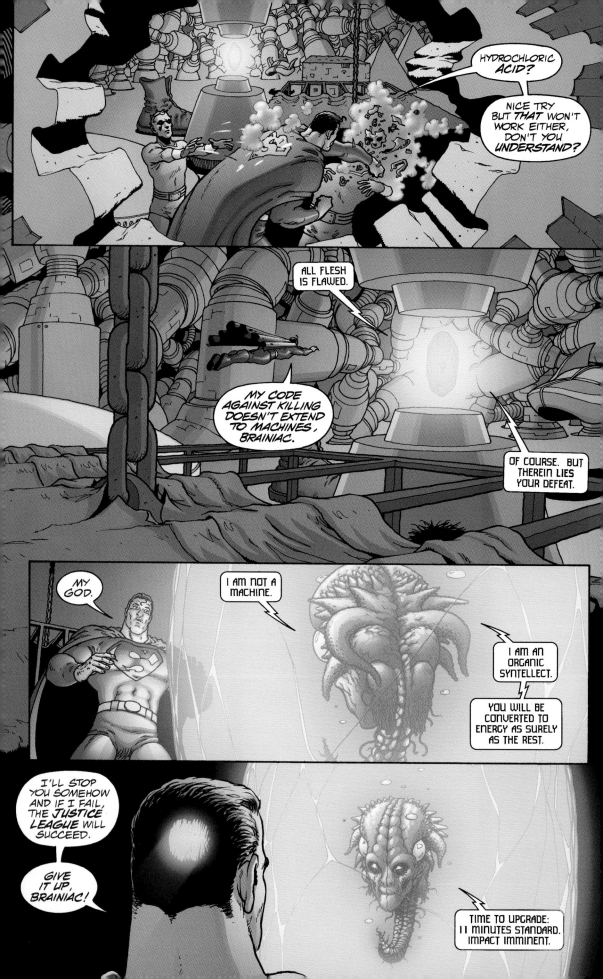

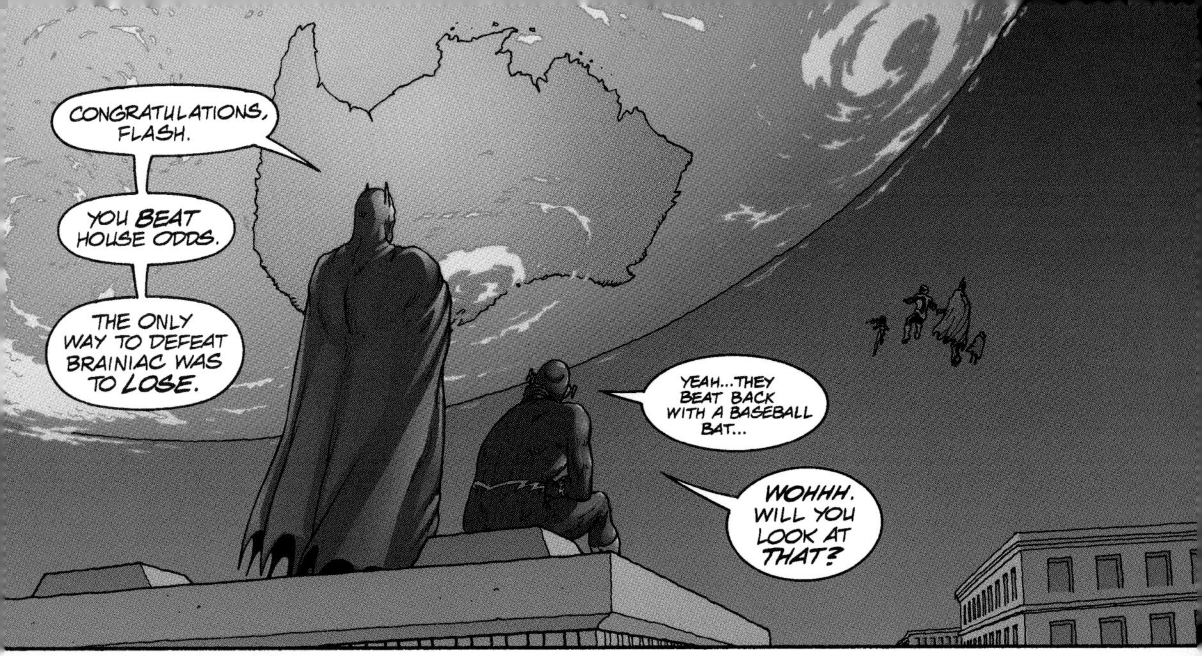
CONGRATULATIONS, FLASH.
YOU BEAT HOUSE ODDS.
THE ONLY WAY TO DEFEAT BRAINIAC WAS TO LOSE.
YEAH...THEY BEAT BACK WITH A BASEBALL BAT...
WOHHH. WILL YOU LOOK AT THAT?

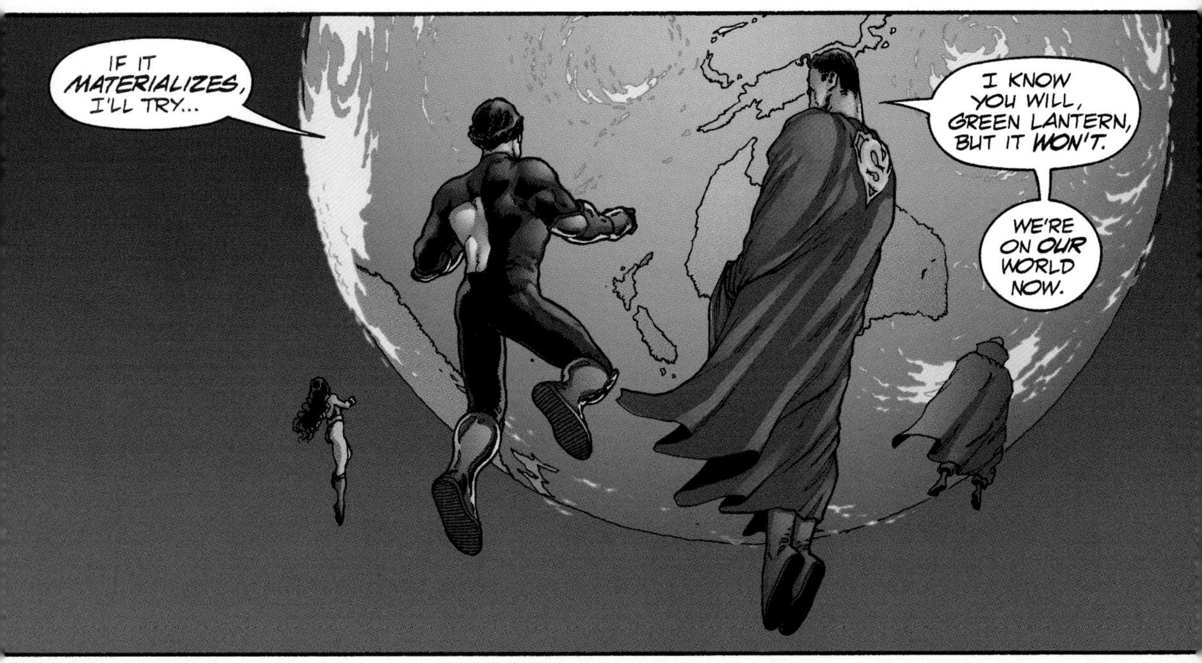
IF IT MATERIALIZES, I'LL TRY...
I KNOW YOU WILL, GREEN LANTERN, BUT IT WON'T.
WE'RE ON OUR WORLD NOW.

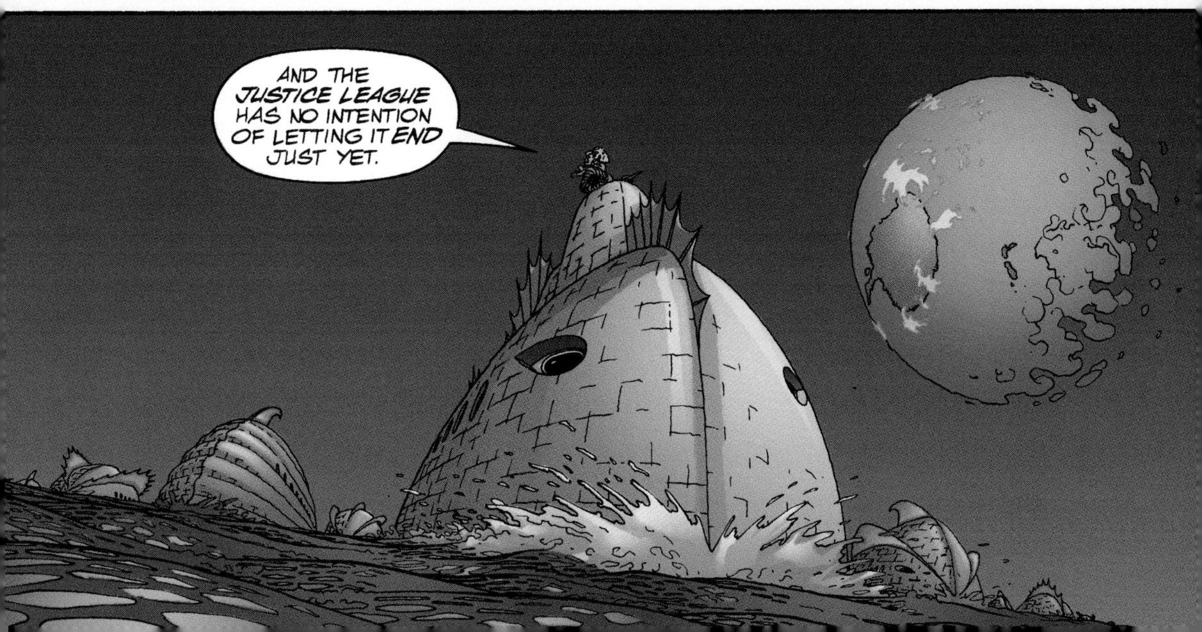
AND THE JUSTICE LEAGUE HAS NO INTENTION OF LETTING IT END JUST YET.

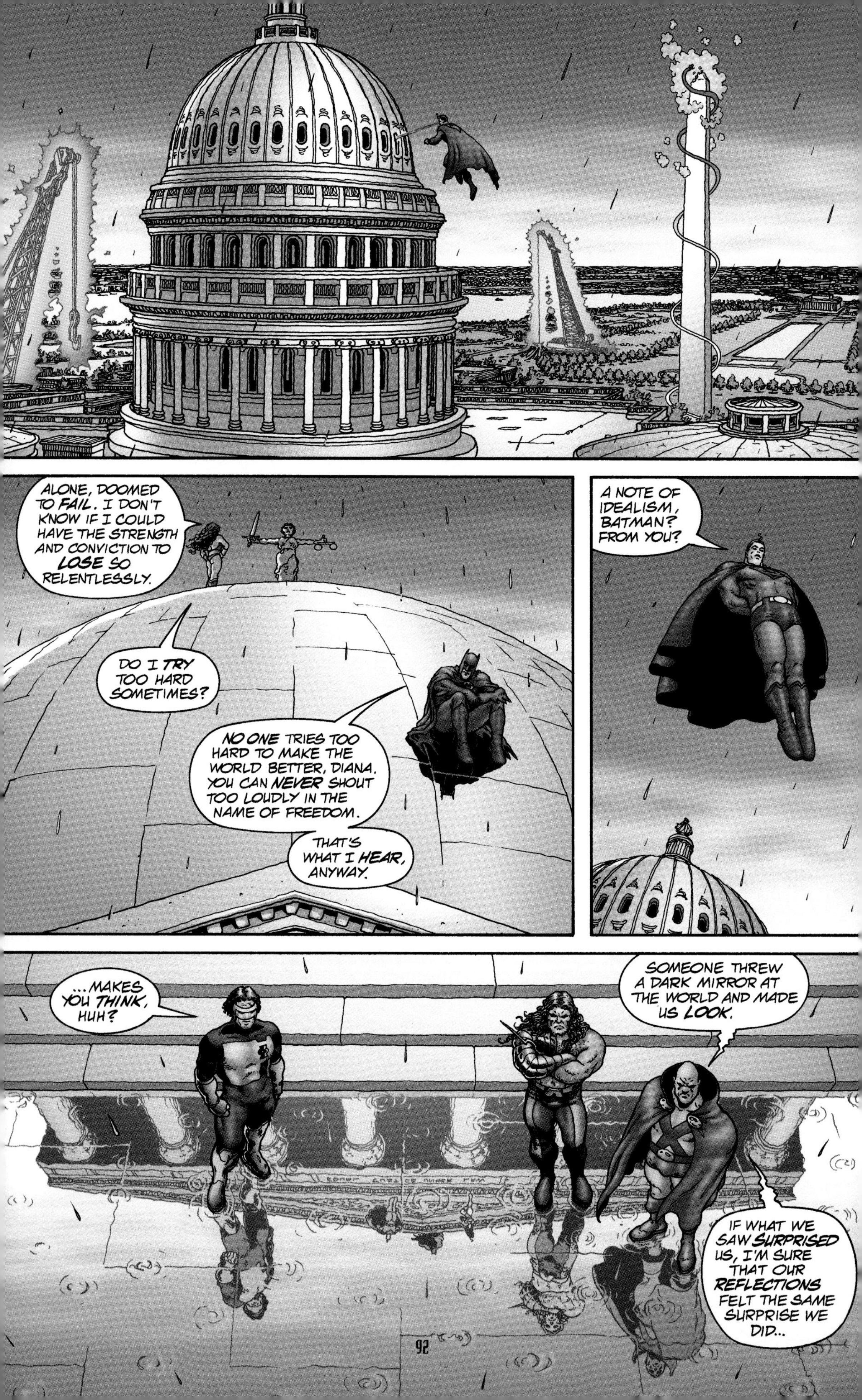

ALONE, DOOMED TO FAIL. I DON'T KNOW IF I COULD HAVE THE STRENGTH AND CONVICTION TO LOSE SO RELENTLESSLY.
DO I TRY TOO HARD SOMETIMES?
NO ONE TRIES TOO HARD TO MAKE THE WORLD BETTER, DIANA. YOU CAN NEVER SHOUT TOO LOUDLY IN THE NAME OF FREEDOM.
THAT'S WHAT I HEAR, ANYWAY.
A NOTE OF IDEALISM, BATMAN? FROM YOU?
...MAKES YOU THINK, HUH?
SOMEONE THREW A DARK MIRROR AT THE WORLD AND MADE US LOOK.
IF WHAT WE SAW SURPRISED US, I'M SURE THAT OUR REFLECTIONS FELT THE SAME SURPRISE WE DID...

...I KEEP THINKING ABOUT *LUTHOR.*

YOUR SUPER-HEARING MUST BE FAILING.

JUST SAYING I'VE *NOTICED* SOMETHING ABOUT PEOPLE WHO TRY TO CHANGE THE WORLD...

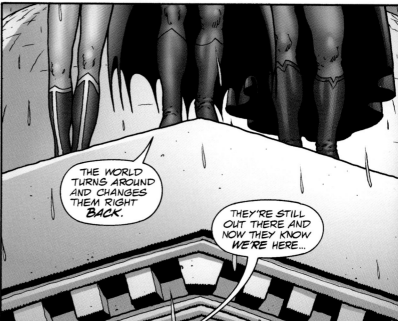

THE WORLD TURNS AROUND AND CHANGES THEM RIGHT *BACK.*

THEY'RE STILL OUT THERE AND NOW THEY KNOW *WE'RE* HERE...

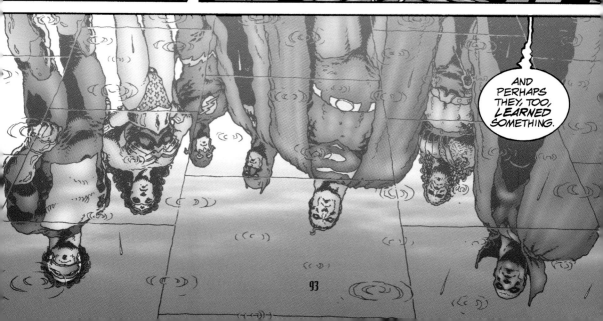

AND PERHAPS THEY, TOO, *LEARNED* SOMETHING.

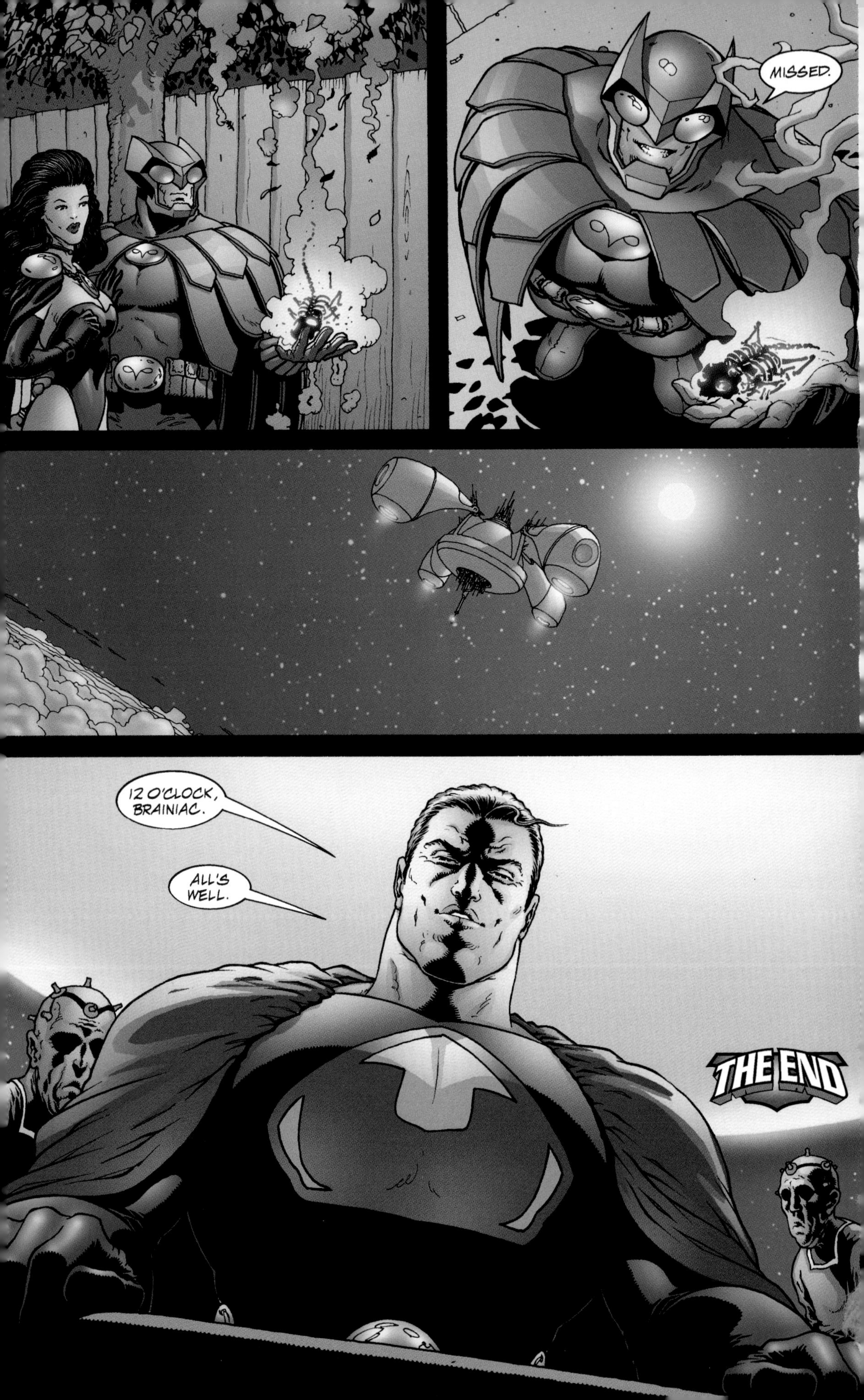
MISSED.
12 O'CLOCK, BRAINIAC.
ALL'S WELL.
THE END